PRAISE FOR THE PLAYS OF NEIL LABUTE

REASONS TO BE HAPPY

"Mr. LaBute is more relaxed as a playwright than he's ever been. He is clearly having a good time revisiting old friends . . . you're likely to feel the same way . . . the most winning romantic comedy of the summer, replete with love talk, LaBute-style, which isn't so far from hate talk . . . "
—**Ben Brantley**, *The New York Times*

"These working-class characters are in fine, foul-mouthed voice, thanks to the scribe's astonishing command of the sharp side of the mother tongue. But this time the women stand up for themselves and give as good as they get."
—**Marilyn Stasio**, *Variety*

"LaBute has a keen ear for conversational dialogue in all its profane, funny and inelegant glory."   —**Joe Dziemianowicz**, *New York Daily News*

"LaBute . . . nails the bad faith, the grasping at straws, the defensive barbs that mark a tasty brawl."   —**Elisabeth Vincentelli**, *New York Post*

". . . intense, funny, and touching . . . In following up with the lives of his earlier characters, LaBute presents another compassionate examination of the ways people struggle to connect and try to find happiness."
—**Jennifer Farrar**, The Associated Press

". . . terrifically entertaining."   —**Philip Boroff**, *Bloomberg*

"[A] triumph . . . always electric with life. LaBute has a terrific way of demonstrating that even in their direst spoken punches . . . fighting lovers are hilarious. . . . completely convincing."   —**David Finkle**, *Huffington Post*

REASONS TO BE PRETTY

"Mr. LaBute is writing some of the freshest and most illuminating American dialogue to be heard anywhere these days . . . Reasons flows with the compelling naturalness of overheard conversation. you mean, or to know what you mean to begin its crude vocabulary, *Reasons to be Pretty* cele the struggle to find out."   —**Ben**

"[T]here is no doubt that LaBute knows how to hold an audience. . . . LaBute proves just as interesting writing about human decency as when he is writing about the darker urgings of the human heart." —**Charles Spencer**, *Telegraph*

"[F]unny, daring, thought-provoking . . ." —**Sarah Hemming**, *Financial Times*

IN A DARK DARK HOUSE

"Refreshingly reminds us . . . that [LaBute's] talents go beyond glibly vicious storytelling and extend into thoughtful analyses of a world rotten with original sin." —**Ben Brantley**, *The New York Times*

"LaBute takes us to shadowy places we don't like to talk about, sometimes even to think about . . ." —**Erin McClam**, *Newsday*

WRECKS

"Superb and subversive . . . A masterly attempt to shed light on the ways in which we manufacture our own darkness. It offers us the kind of illumination that Tom Stoppard has called 'what's left of God's purpose when you take away God.'" —**John Lahr**, *The New Yorker*

"[*Wrecks* is a] tasty morsel of a play . . . The profound empathy that has always informed LaBute's work, even at its most stringent, is expressed more directly and urgently than ever here." —**Elysa Gardner**, *USA Today*

"*Wrecks* is bound to be identified by its shock value. But it must also be cherished for the moment-by-moment pleasure of its masterly portraiture. There is not an extraneous syllable in LaBute's enormously moving love story." —**Linda Winer**, *Newsday*

FAT PIG

"The most emotionally engaging and unsettling of Mr. LaBute's plays since *bash* . . . A serious step forward for a playwright who has always been most comfortable with judgmental distance." —**Ben Brantley**, *The New York Times*

"One of Neil LaBute's subtler efforts . . . Demonstrates a warmth and compassion for its characters missing in many of LaBute's previous works [and] balances black humor and social commentary in a . . . beautifully written, hilarious . . . dissection of how societal pressures affect relationships [that] is astute and up-to-the-minute relevant." —**Frank Scheck**, *New York Post*

THE DISTANCE FROM HERE

"LaBute gets inside the emptiness of American culture, the masquerade, and the evil of neglect. *The Distance from Here*, it seems to me, is a new title to be added to the short list of important contemporary plays."

—**John Lahr**, *The New Yorker*

THE MERCY SEAT

"Though set in the cold, gray light of morning in a downtown loft with inescapable views of the vacuum left by the twin towers, *The Mercy Seat* really occurs in one of those feverish nights of the soul in which men and women lock in vicious sexual combat, as in Strindberg's *Dance of Death* and Edward Albee's *Who's Afraid of Virginia Woolf*." —**Ben Brantley**, *The New York Times*

"[A] powerful drama . . . LaBute shows a true master's hand in gliding us amid the shoals and reefs of a mined relationship." —**Donald Lyons**, *New York Post*

THE SHAPE OF THINGS

"LaBute . . . continues to probe the fascinating dark side of individualism . . . [His] great gift is to live in and to chronicle that murky area of not-knowing, which mankind spends much of its waking life denying."

—**John Lahr**, *The New Yorker*

"LaBute is the first dramatist since David Mamet and Sam Shepard—since Edward Albee, actually—to mix sympathy and savagery, pathos and power."

—**Donald Lyons**, *New York Post*

"*Shape* . . . is LaBute's thesis on extreme feminine wiles, as well as a disquisition on how far an artist . . . can go in the name of art . . . Like a chiropractor of the soul, LaBute is looking for realignment, listening for a crack." —**John Istel**, *Elle*

BASH

"The three stories in *bash* are correspondingly all, in different ways, about the power instinct, about the animalistic urge for control. In rendering these narratives, Mr. LaBute shows not only a merciless ear for contemporary speech but also a poet's sense of recurring, slyly graduated imagery . . . darkly engrossing."

—**Ben Brantley**, *The New York Times*

NEIL LABUTE is an award-winning playwright, filmmaker, and screen-writer. His plays include: *bash*, *The Shape of Things*, *The Distance From Here*, *The Mercy Seat*, *Fat Pig* (Olivier Award nominated for Best Comedy), *Some Girl(s)*, *Reasons to be Pretty* (Tony Award nominated for Best Play), *In A Forest, Dark and Deep*, a new adaptation of *Miss Julie,* and *Reasons to be Happy.* He is also the author of *Seconds of Pleasure*, a collection of short fiction, and a 2013 recipient of a Literature Award from the American Academy of Arts and Letters.

Neil LaBute's films include *In the Company of Men* (New York Critics' Circle Award for Best First Feature and the Filmmaker Trophy at the Sundance Film Festival), *Your Friends and Neighbors*, *Nurse Betty*, *Possession*, *The Shape of Things*, *Lakeview Terrace*, *Death at a Funeral, Some Velvet Morning*, and *Dirty Weekend.*

Some
Velvet Morning

a play by

Neil LaBute

THE OVERLOOK PRESS
NEW YORK, NY

First published in the United States in 2014 by
The Overlook Press, Peter Mayer Publishers, Inc.

141 Wooster Street
New York, NY 10012
www.overlookpress.com
For bulk and special sales, please contact sales@overlookny.com,
or write us at the above address.

Cataloging-in-Publication Data is available from the Library of Congress

Book design and type formatting by Bernard Schleifer
Manufactured in the United States of America
ISBN 978-1-4683-0916-4
1 3 5 7 9 10 8 6 4 2

for august strindberg. with love.

under this mask, another mask.
i will never finish lifting up all these faces.

—CLAUDE CAHUN

they slipped briskly into an intimacy from which they never recovered.

—F. SCOTT FITZGERALD

everything means everything.

—THE NATIONAL

Preface

Anton Chekhov once made a fascinating observation (among a lifetime of fascinating observations, both on and off the page) which amounted to this: "Every person lives his real, most interesting life under the cover of secrecy."

I'm not sure if I completely agree with the above statement, but I do think it's an intriguing idea to consider. How much do we ever really know about a person? Even the folks around us who make up our families or number among our friends: what do we actually know about their hearts and minds or vice versa?

"Precious little" is probably the real answer. Some people are no doubt more open than others, but most of us have a series of selves that we use for any number of situations or relationships, and we keep shifting around these personas in an effort to both keep others happy and ourselves happy, too (along with safe and protected).

Now, I'm no psychologist but I do spend a lot of my time as a writer being an amateur therapist as I create a variety of psychological profiles for people who do not exist but whom I must make extremely believable for my audience of readers or theatergoers. People are very quick today to say "I don't believe that" and stop watching or listening or reading; Dr. Phil and a bevy of other TV personalities have made sure that most people today have at least a layperson's knowledge of how the mind works and what real human behavior should look and sound like, and that's a good thing, as far as I'm concerned. It forces me and other writers to be honest and to keep pushing ourselves to hold a real mirror up to the work we do and to make it as credible as possible.

That said, who doesn't love a good secret?

The script you now have in your hands is an effort on my part to examine a relationship in real-time on stage. I've certainly done this kind of thing before (*The Mercy Seat, In a Forest, Dark and Deep*, and my adaptation of *Miss Julie* being three of the more obvious examples) but I don't think my personal concentration on the moment-to-moment emotional landscape of a couple has ever been more acutely wired to the work than in this particular piece. Theater by its very nature is about being "in the moment," and no matter how many scenes play out across the stage in a given performance, we are obviously watching actors perform in "real time." What I'm talking about here is something else —a desire on my part to connect all of the emotional dots between a man and a woman who find themselves together again after a period of separation (and with a long and twisted personal history behind them). I wanted to try to write all those bits, to put them down on paper and allow some actors to breathe even more vibrant life into them (as they always do). At the same time, however, I wanted to craft a story that was a rollercoaster ride for the reader or the viewer, one that works on a number of levels and while you may in fact recognize it as a ride, my job is to make sure it's one that you've never been on before.

And some of that thrill comes from this idea of "secrets." Information that I or the characters withhold from the audience or from each other, piling possibilities up high, one on top of the other, until the story can be approached and discussed and dissected from a variety of angles. That's what makes it fun to write and to perform and to watch or read or both (I hope). Theater is about what's possible; let life tell you what's impossible—if you choose to spend time with me and my work, then I'm going to give you nothing but possibilities. That doesn't mean any of this stuff is highly probable—go watch a documentary or read the encyclopedia if that's what you're looking for—but if you want to play games and enjoy the stage as a magical place where good and bad and funny and sad play out in marvelous ninety minute bursts, then you've come to the right place. That's what I'm shooting for: magic.

This time, however, I went the long way around. Usually when I write a script like *Some Velvet Morning* it makes the most sense to go straight to the stage and so I'll approach one of a handful of theater companies I've worked with in the past and send them the manuscript. Something held me back with this one. I was at a place in my film career where I had virtually stopped writing and directing new material for the screen; I was a director for hire, adapting books or remaking films or working for someone else to bring another person's vision to the cinemas. Over the last four years I had made a few short films and those renewed my faith in the process; they cost almost nothing to make but I was in control of the content and it felt great. I made them in black & white and I hired people that I wanted to work with and we made these little films without anybody knowing anything about them. Was it a secret? I don't know, but I loved it.

Having done that, it felt like it was time to do the same thing on a bigger scale, and that's where the idea of taking this script to film first was born.

A number of really helpful people came on board to facilitate this, among them the producers Tim Harms and Daryl Freimark, along with producer Michael Corrente, and together we put together a financial package that allowed us to make a film in a very short period of time but with absolute control over both the process and the product. One special financier by the name of Forrest E. Crisman, Jr., became our guardian angel, and I thank him again for taking a risk on such a particular kind of entertainment.

The film version of this script was made in eight days in Park Slope, Brooklyn, and it was a blast to work on (a ninth day was partially used in a studio in Brooklyn to fulfill an obligation for the New York State tax rebate and that is what helped create our unique overhead title sequence).

The characters of Fred and Velvet were played by Stanley Tucci and Alice Eve and they are not solely but primarily responsible for the film's success. The film lives or dies by those two characters, and in these two actors I found the most fabulous and fearless collaborators. We had three days of rehearsal (or what some people might refer to as "nothing") and in that short period of time we mercilessly attacked the script, ripping out some twenty pages or more. That is why this published version contains many passages that are not included in the film—two different mediums, each ultimately requiring a different kind of text.

I'm thrilled with what we captured on film (thanks to the astonishing eye of the director of photography, Rogier Stoffers, whom I've been lucky enough to work with four times now) but I can't wait to see this piece fully realized on the stage as well. Occasionally a close-up of Stanley or Alice humbles me and reminds me of the great and powerful purpose of cinema—to study the human face. That said, to see this story played out on a stage by two actors, from the start of the tale through to the raw and upsetting physical demands of the climax, will be a unique pleasure. There is nothing quite like the theater, and that's why we keep coming back (and why it will never die, much to the chagrin of the naysayers—many of whom have now taken to tweeting their negative thoughts rather than writing them down in fully formed sentences like adults do).

One other thing worth mentioning is the dedication to August Strindberg. I have a number of influences in my writing life and on this project in particular—Ingmar Bergman's *Scenes from a Marriage* was an obvious one along with a host of other films and plays—but Strindberg is the granddaddy of them all and so I wanted to tip my hat in his general direction. I was recently in Stockholm at their film festival presenting the *Velvet* film, and I got a chance to visit the Strindberg Museum, which is housed in his last place of residence in that beautiful city. I was humbled and moved (and I sat on the bed that he passed away in but don't tell anyone).

So this text is now what it is: first just words on a page and then a film and now a play—not the usual journey for me but one that's been exciting and worth the trip. This script should be taken for what it is but with the knowledge that its foundation is built on secrets and that's nothing to be afraid of. Secrets, like lies, are things that often lead us to the truth, and that's what we all seek—on the stage and in our lives. We continually look for the truth but like this script, we sometimes take the long way around.

Writing is tough. I'll never believe that I've mastered it and some days I barely feel like I know what I'm doing (and I've been at this for twenty years now, this writing thing) but I do know that the answers are out there and when we search and we don't find them, sometimes we have to make them up for ourselves. We have to write new answers and ask new questions.

That's the job. It's what I do. Stay tuned.

Neil LaBute
November 2013

Some Velvet Morning

An alternative version of this text was made into a feature film starring Stanley Tucci and Alice Eve and directed by the author.

Silence. Darkness.

I'll write all this stuff later. It just doesn't matter that much. It's a room we're in. A nice big apartment in a city somewhere.

WOMAN (20s) sitting. Maybe listening to music or could just be reading. Doorbell rings. She checks her watch.

She goes to a door. MAN (50s) standing there. Suitcases.

FRED . . . so "hi." It's me. (Beat.) Fred.

VELVET Oh. Hey. (*Beat.*) Ummmm, wow. Hello there.

FRED I'm here. If that's ok. I'm here with all my stuff and I'd like to . . . anyway. Yes. I came here with it.

VELVET Ok . . .

FRED I brought it to your place. With me.

VELVET I see that.

FRED Tell me to go if you want to, but . . .

VELVET No, no. God, that's not, no. I'm just . . .

FRED Surprise!

VELVET Yeah! It's quite the . . . yes. A surprise. (*Beat.*) So, is your plane not something? Is it delayed or what? I don't get it.

FRED No, that's not . . . I'm here. To see you. To maybe, I dunno, see what we can—is it ok if I come in?

VELVET Ummmm, sure. Yes. You can't stand out on the landing all day so, yeah, come in. I have to go out soon, but we can . . . yes.

He doesn't hesitate—heads straight inside with his gear.

FRED Great. I didn't know what you'd think . . . and I didn't wanna just, you know, so I thought about calling and then trying to explain and all that and, and, that's a real—how do you explain away *fifty*-some years of a life over the phone? Right? I don't have a calling plan that'll support that! (*Tries to laugh.*) That's meant to be a joke but it was just stupid instead, so I'm sorry. I feel nervous.

VELVET Why?

FRED I dunno. I just am.

VELVET Well, there's certainly nothing to feel—we know each other, Fred. Have for a long time. No reason for either of us to feel bad about things. At all.

FRED I know. I know that, but I still do. Not bad, I didn't say that. I said "nervous."

VELVET Ok.

FRED Is that alright?

VELVET Of course.

FRED Good.

VELVET However you wanna feel is fine. It's ok.

FRED Great. Thank you.

VELVET But so . . . seriously, though, are you going somewhere or what? That is a lot of stuff ya got there!

FRED Yeah. It's everything I could carry. Or talk people into carrying for me! On the plane, I mean—you can only carry on two things or whatever, bags, and I'd already sent the big ones through, these two. (*Pointing.*) And so I've got all these smaller cases and grocery bags—I just grabbed a bunch of crap at home, anything that was mine or at all made sense and I got outta there. Did it while Miriam was out at the store! Can you imagine?! What a coward I am. Seriously. Twenty-*seven* years of being married to the woman and that's how I go. Like that. Like some neighborhood kid who got in through a basement window and running around the place shoving *valuables* into pillowcases! I make myself sick. Really. But hey, here I am. (*Beat.*) Anyhow I had to ask a few of my fellow travelers if they could pretend that some of this shit was theirs so that I could—which is totally against airline policy but I did it and— you know. Yeah.

VELVET Huh. That's . . . maybe you should call her.

FRED Who?

VELVET Your wife.

FRED Oh, right. Yes, maybe so. I mean, no, I definitely will, at some point.

VELVET And Chris? What about him?

FRED Ha! (*Thinking.*) What about him?

VELVET Well, ummmm . . . he's your son, for one thing, so he's probably gonna want to know what's up. I would. And he's . . .
I mean, you being here, at my home? I don't think that's gonna
make all that much sense to him.

FRED Probably not. (*Beat.*) Could I have water?

VELVET Sure. (*Beat.*) I don't think he'll like it.

FRED True. Not that he has to find out.

VELVET Still.

FRED Yeah. Well, in a strange way, I suppose he was the one who
introduced us . . . or . . .

VELVET *Fred* . . .

FRED No, I mean, at least kinda.

VELVET *I* introduced us. It wasn't him.

FRED I know, I know, I'm just saying . . .

VELVET It was *me*. I put a note in your pocket, so it wasn't him.

FRED Yeah, but if he hadn't been seeing you . . .

VELVET That's—I'm not gonna let you put this on him. It's not fair.

FRED No, I'm not, I just mean that his . . . him going out with you
prompted it, that's all.

VELVET No, not true. Come on.

FRED I'm not saying he'll understand this and be all happy for me! I'm not saying that. Alright? I just mean that he's . . .

VELVET He still sees me, from time to time. Ok? We have lunch and, and . . . so, I'm not at all sure he's gonna be very . . . you know what I'm saying! You know exactly.

FRED You do? Lunch? Really? With "wonder boy?"

VELVET Sometimes. Sometimes other things.

FRED Oh. Huh. "Other things." Ok. (*Beat.*) He's married now, ya know. In case he didn't mention it. We have a habit in our family of forgetting to mention shit like that. Important shit, like our age, or . . . or . . . "marriage."

VELVET Well, yes, he is. And he did.

FRED Ok. And yet he's . . . *really*? So is Mandy aware of this? (*Beat.*) Mandy's his wife . . .

VELVET I know. (*Beat.*) I'd guess not but I'm not that deep a part of his life so I don't really know. Or care.

FRED That's fine, I just . . . I bet she doesn't.

VELVET I'd guess the same. (*Gives him water.*) So here. Take it.

FRED Thanks. My mouth is so dry—from the very second I started this, grabbing my things off the shelves, I've had this crazy sort of dryness in my throat and I can't seem to get rid of it. No matter what I do.

VELVET Huh.

FRED Asked the girl on the plane about a dozen times for water and juice—a *beer*, even!—to try and get rid of it but it just kept hanging there in the back of my throat. A kind of . . . what else can you call it? (*Drinks.*) This real deserty-sort of dryness.

VELVET Do you feel sick or anything? Maybe you caught something recently and it's now just starting to . . .

FRED No, I don't think so. I'm gonna sit, is that ok? (*He sits.*) Just while I . . .

VELVET Ummmmm, sure. Go ahead. I *do* need to get ready in a little bit, but you can . . .

FRED Yeah, you said that. You're going out.

VELVET I am. This morning.

FRED That's great. Good. (*Beat.*) Where to?

VELVET Oh, you know. Day off and I'm . . . shopping.

FRED Yeah? (*Beat.*) Aren't they all sorta "days off" for you? I mean, you don't really have a proper—nothing. But do you? Not that I know about . . .

VELVET No, I don't. Not a "proper" one, no.

FRED Well, we can't *all* be lawyers; there'd be nobody left to hate! (*Beat.*) But anyway, you're going out. *Shopping.*

VELVET A little bit, probably. That and seeing a friend. *Friends.* Something like that.

FRED Great. Ok. That's fine.

VELVET Uh-huh.

FRED But nothing specific?

VELVET No. (*Beat.*) I mean, no, I didn't say that. I said—yes, somewhat specific. Lunch.

FRED Yeah? Really?

VELVET *Yes*, Fred. I'm not just—there are people who are expecting to hear from me soon.

FRED I'm not calling you a liar. I just asked a question.

VELVET Ok, then. (*Beat.*) So . . . anyway, what about you? What is all this?

FRED Yeah. Can you believe it? I mean, me and this whole thing? "Leaving."

VELVET It's wild . . .

FRED I know! God, I can't even wrap my—don't be afraid or anything. You can sit, too. I'm excited about stuff, maybe a little bit wound up, but I'm not dangerous. Sit.

VELVET No, I'm fine, I've just . . . I *exercised* a little while ago and I'm all . . .

FRED Why don't you sit so we can talk?

VELVET It's fine, we're talking.

FRED Please. Just sit.

VELVET Fred, I'm really fine, I'd rather . . .

FRED SIT! (*Beat.*) Sorry, I'm not . . . but please. It makes me nervous, you standing there, like you're *timing* me or something.

VELVET I'm not. Promise.

FRED I know that, of course I know that, in a rational way I get it, but me sitting on the couch and you just standing there and tapping you fingers on your . . . it's making me edgy. I'm sorry.

VELVET No problem. I can sit. (*She does.*) There. Now we can talk. I wasn't trying to make you feel rushed or anything, not at all. I just do have some—anyway. I'm sitting.

FRED Good.

VELVET Sure.

FRED Thank you.

VELVET Of course. Sorry to make you feel . . .

FRED You didn't. That's what I was saying to you, that you weren't, I mean rationally you weren't, but it just felt like it a bit. I "felt" like you were sorta trying to push me back out the door. At least in your mind.

VELVET No. I wasn't. I wouldn't do that to you— you know that.

FRED I do know. Obviously.

VELVET I'm not that kind of person.

FRED Yes, but in my head. That's where I felt it and you standing over me didn't help it at all. So . . . (*Beat.*) Doesn't matter now 'cause you're sitting. Even though you keep checking your watch . . .

She acknowledges this even as she checks her watch again.

VELVET Sorry! I just do have . . . some . . .

FRED I know, I get it! I'm not supposed to be here. You weren't expecting me . . . (*Beat.*) You've made that pretty damn clear now, so can we just . . . move on to some other . . .

VELVET I mean, I really wasn't. It's a surprise.

FRED Good one, I hope.

VELVET . . . of course. A shock, even. But good.

FRED Really? Is it?

VELVET Yes. It is.

FRED Ok. Good. Great! I'm glad.

VELVET Me, too. I mean, to see you.

FRED Yeah. It's been awhile.

VELVET Uh-huh. Years, actually.

FRED That's true. I did what I said, what I'd promised you I would do. I stayed away. And it was not easy all the time, I mean, in the beginning, right after we broke up—that was hell. Living with it. No one to talk about it with. But I did it.

VELVET Right. And I appreciate that . . .

FRED I mean, there were a few calls and those emails that we'd send, back and forth—maybe I gave you a birthday present one year, didn't I? That iPod thingie, with your name *engraved* on it?— but mostly I stayed away. Like you asked me to.

VELVET Thank you. I mean, for being a gentleman.

FRED Ha! I don't know about that! But yeah. I did what I said I'd do. For a long time.

VELVET Thanks. (*Beat.*) *So* . . .

FRED Yeah. And that's an understatement! "So!" So what the hell do I do *now*? Huh?

VELVET Ummmm . . .

FRED Honestly. What?

VELVET I mean . . . you're not seriously asking my advice here, are you? Because . . . I'm . . .

FRED Kind of. Yes.

VELVET I'm not in a really good position to help you with that, Fred. Ya know? I mean, you just show up here, *twenty* bags scattered at your feet—I don't have answers for a puzzle like that one. (*Beat.*) I think you should go to a hotel and settle in—maybe call your wife, like I said, and then eat something, get a good rest—but otherwise I'd just be making up crap if I told you what to do, gave you any type of advice. Only you know why you've done this— all the little things that led you to do it—I really don't know what else to say.

FRED Ok.

VELVET I'd like to help you but I can't.

FRED It's alright! I didn't expect for you to sort out all the . . . whatever . . . *shit* I've gotten myself into, I wouldn't ask that of you. I promise.

VELVET Fine then. Good.

FRED Just thought you might throw out an *idea* or two, that sorta thing. But hey—

VELVET I told you to call your wife . . .

FRED Gee, thanks!

VELVET Well . . .

FRED What good is that gonna do? Huh? Make me say the words, is that it? "I left you." Is that what I should—I think she gets it! The empty closet should be a fairly strong indication that it wasn't, like, the *rapture* or anything . . .

VELVET Ok, then maybe you should—you oughta do what you wanna do, then.

FRED I wanna be here.

VELVET Ummmmm . . . alright . . .

FRED I mean, if that's what you're asking, is for me to do exactly what *I* want to do or be in that place that *I* really want to be in, then this is it. Here. With you. And you know that I've never done that—least for any length of time—thought about me or my needs first in this. I haven't. No. I've always done the "right" thing; gone back to my wife and stopped seeing you . . . let my kid live the life he wanted to and try not to be too intrusive about that, be a nice I dunno what, co-worker to my fellow whomevers—I've been a good guy! Mostly . . . at least sort-of. Or a decent guy, maybe that's a better way to put it—"good" is tricky, kind of elusive to me, but I've been very decent with people. I have . . . (*Beat.*) Right?

VELVET . . . I'm not disagreeing . . .

FRED Yeah, but you're not exactly waving a flag in my direction either! I could really use a little support here today . . . (*Beat.*) Sorry! I'm just . . .

VELVET I agree with you, Fred. Alright? Is that enough?

FRED It's fine.

VELVET Good.

FRED Don't say it if you don't mean it.

VELVET I won't.

FRED Or, you know, "feel" it or something. If you don't then just say it. Say it to me.

VELVET Stop being *so*—please, ok? You're being a little . . . bit . . .

FRED What?

VELVET I dunno! Pushy about this or . . . not pushy, you know I don't mean that, but charged up about things. (*Beat.*) The way you're just staring and . . . you know, talking at me with this edge to your voice, going a mile a minute—it's a little unnerving. Just try and, you know, just let it be.

He nods, watching her as she fidgets a bit in her chair.

FRED Hey, I'm not The Beatles, ok? I can't be *cool* all the time . . . (*Beat.*) That's meant to be a joke also. Ouch! I'm striking out here.

VELVET I figured. That is was a joke, I mean.

FRED Sorry. I'm just—what time do you have to go? If you need to shower or anything I'm fine to just sit here and . . . you know. I'd be ok with that.

VELVET No, it's not . . . that's . . .

FRED I've seen you in a towel before, so don't worry about it. Go ahead if you need to.

VELVET I'm good on time. Really.

FRED I've had the whole damn thing, honey, so don't be bashful! Go *douche* if you're in a hurry. That's . . .

VELVET Fred. I'm fine, I said. I might throw on some different clothes, but otherwise . . .

FRED Well alright then. You oughta know. Isn't that right?

VELVET Yes.

FRED You should know your schedule lots better than me. Or say, *Chris*. Isn't that true?

VELVET I should. Yep.

FRED And how is Chris? If I may ask? How's is the "wonder boy" doing?

VELVET He's doing pretty well, I think. I mean, last time I saw him, which was . . .

FRED When?

VELVET . . . I was just about to say . . .

FRED Sorry.

VELVET You don't have to keep saying "sorry" about everything. Fred.

FRED *Sorry.* (*Beat.*) Damnit! Sorry about that . . . about being "sorry." Or saying it. Ok?

VELVET Don't worry about it. (*Puts a hand on his leg.*) Just relax. It's all . . . fine.

FRED Thanks. (*Beat.*) God, that feels good! So, so good. Your hand there. Your touch.

He continues to touch her, pulling her closer and closer. She allows it for a moment but finally stops him.

VELVET Ok, I'm glad, but that's not why I . . .

FRED I know! You were comforting me and not trying to be all *sexy* or whatever, I'm not stupid . . . I'm just saying . . .

VELVET . . . nobody's calling you anything . . .

FRED Feels great. That's all I'm saying. It's not loaded with personal meaning . . .

VELVET Fine. Just trying to be clear about . . .

FRED I just reacted to it! I'm that kind of a person, reactive, and I react when I feel a sensation that's good or bad. That is a part of me and I'm not gonna apologize to you for it. I can't do that.

VELVET I'm not asking for that. I wouldn't just *assume* it, ok, so please don't be . . .

FRED Fine! Let's stop, please, my nerves are so shot today and I want you to see me at my very best, not in some horrible . . .

VELVET . . . it's ok . . . honestly, it's . . .

FRED No, Velvet, it is not "ok" or I would've said so, alright? If things were all ok I think I'd be able to pick up on a deal like that—"all is well"—and say so. I'd be saying "things are ok" instead of "now what the hell's going on?" So this is not exactly an "ok" moment for me! OK?

VELVET O-K. (*Beat.*) That's me trying to be funny now . . .

FRED Ha! (*Laughs.*) Ho-ho-ho. No, you're right, that feels great, to get it all out in a big rush of laughter like that, thanks . . . guess I'll be on my way now. (*He stands.*) Thanks so much for having me over and for helping me out. You're so, so great and you've really put me back on track . . .

VELVET You're not—you didn't mean any of that, did you? (*Beat.*) What you just said there. You don't mean it at all . . .

FRED Not even one word of it.

VELVET I could tell.

FRED Well then terrific! I've still got it . . . the ol' way with words. It's a real gift.

VELVET I don't know what I said to make you so angry, Fred . . . but . . .

FRED I'm not angry.

VELVET You kinda are. Right now. *Aggressive.*

FRED A little. Ok, yes, maybe a little.

VELVET Well, however much it feels to you—some or a bunch or

just a touch—it's coming off you in waves, alright? Big tsunami
waves of anger and they're hitting me so hard in the chest that
I . . . I dunno what . . . I feel ready to start crying as I sit here.
I could start weeping this instant . . . if that's what you're looking
for. (*Beat.*) Just being honest.

FRED That's not what I . . . shit, I'm sorry! I'm so so sorry. Velvet.
I am. Please . . . (*He sits.*) Obviously I didn't come here to do that.
Or to say "sorry." Shit. Sorry!

VELVET It's ok, I'm not . . . look, I understand . . . but . . .

FRED Please do. *Please.*

VELVET I do, but it's so, you know . . . there's a whole lot of history
here and it's very easy for it to spill over . . . to just . . .

FRED I know . . . (*Pats her leg.*) I can see how it might feel like that,
me being angry, now that you say something, and I'm asking if
you'll forgive me. That was dumb of me to just *waltz* in here and—
will you? Please?

VELVET Of course.

FRED Thanks. Thank you very much. (*Beat.*) I'm really serious,
though. Please please do forgive me, Velvet.

VELVET I am, Fred. I'm forgiving you right now. (*Beat.*) And please
don't do that, ok?

FRED What? What're you . . . ?

VELVET "Velvet." Don't keep calling me that.

FRED Really?

VELVET You know that's not—why would I want you doing that now, years later and I am not that girl any more—that's no longer me so please respect that. Ok?

FRED Ummm, ok, but . . . (*Beat.*) Actually, no.

VELVET What's "no?"

FRED I'm not so sure that's true.

VELVET Excuse me? Excuse me, Fred, but how the fuck would you know if I'm doing a thing in my life or not? Seriously, tell me . . . unless you're here and me and doing the day-to-day of what I do—just how do you have any answer to that?

FRED Because of what you said. That's how.

VELVET And what was that? Hmmm? I said what?

FRED About Chris.

VELVET *What*?

FRED My son. Chris. The guy you used to go out with and you now see in private—I guess that's what led me to believe it. That little fact.

VELVET I said I see him for "lunch" sometimes.

FRED And other stuff! You said that, too.

VELVET I didn't mean . . .

FRED You said "sometimes other stuff." What in the hell does that mean if not—obviously you were implying that you guys are . . .

VELVET I didn't mean *that*!

FRED Oh, yeah? Really? You said it a couple minutes ago, you practically *threw* it in my face so I'm pretty sure I'm not making it up. The implications of it . . .

VELVET No, that's, *no*, what I said was . . .

FRED Oh God, let's argue *semantics*, fine . . . that'll make the trip from Baltimore worth it, if you and I can get into a big argument about the meaning of some words. I hate words! Hate. Them. They are a pain in the ass and the reason for, I'm not sure but . . . maybe half of the things wrong with America. *Words*. (*Beat*.) Sounds great, go for it. Can't wait. "Velvet."

VELVET I am not "Velvet" anymore so stop it!

FRED *You* stop! You're the one yelling at me!

VELVET Yeah, because you're . . . you keep . . . !

FRED So stop then! Stop it!!

VELVET I am. I'm stopping now and it's because this is ridiculous. What we're allowing ourselves to do here. Act like children.

They back away from each other for a moment—taking up a pair of different positions in the room.

FRED Hey, children are underrated. They get it like nobody else— they totally get what's going on in most situations, whether they can do anything about it or not, they do "get" it. So . . . just . . .

VELVET Look, Fred, what I meant was . . . maybe you are just, I dunno, wrapping all this up in what's happening in your home life or something, and that's alright, I can see how that might— but I don't like to hear that name anymore, it's not me or anyone that I associate with myself and if Chris was here he'd tell you the same thing . . . he really would. Or anybody else that I'm seeing in my life.

FRED "Seeing." I like that. It's so proper! I love that you give it a name like that: "I'm seeing someone."

VELVET Yes, *seeing*, as in a quick drink with or friendly and maybe us going to a film or whatever—so yes, I'm in a place where I have what I'd call actual friends or even boyfriends . . . nothing really serious, but that's good, it's cool, it's what I need right now. Space. Freedom. I want a lot of just plain ol' "me" time so I can do what I'm doing which is school and art and, and . . . I dunno what! Finding myself, alright? For the first time in a really long time—as *mystical* and bullshitty as that sounds, that is what I'm up to these days and nobody calls me "Velvet." (*Beat.*) So I'm asking you nicely not to.

FRED Great. I can do that. It's just a word . . .

VELVET That's true.

FRED Just something I associate with you but I can easily change that around and I'll . . . so what're you going by, then? If I may ask?

VELVET I dunno. I mean, it doesn't matter. (*Beat.*) I really do need to get—

FRED I'm not stopping you.

VELVET No, yeah, you kinda are, Fred. In a big way. (*Beat.*) May not feel like it but you are putting a huge block in my road. Ok?

FRED Really?

VELVET I don't wanna be rude, but yes. This is now starting to make me . . . I dunno what. Worried, I guess. Having you here.

FRED Huh. Sorry. (*Beat.*) How'd you get that name, anyway?

VELVET Which?

FRED Come on! *Velvet.* Where'd that come from? I don't think I ever asked you before or I can't remember, at least. So where?

VELVET . . . I dunno.

FRED Of course you do!

VELVET Not really—I just started using it.

FRED Bull. That's—was it a nickname some guy gave you? Hmmm? Or maybe . . .

VELVET Nope.

FRED Really? It's not for the way your snatch feels when it wraps around a guy's thing? I'd believe it if you told me that . . .

VELVET Please don't say shit like—sorry. No.

FRED Or your mouth, maybe? How that tongue of yours works when it's sliding up and down the shaft of my—feels like you wrapped one 'a those Elvis paintings around me and are moving it back and forth! Your lips are that nice.

VELVET I suppose that's meant to be a compliment or something . . .

FRED Pretty much. Yes.

VELVET Huh. Ok. So were you thinking about me or Elvis as I was doing it?

FRED You. Usually.

VELVET Asshole!

FRED Ha! I'm kidding. All but one time. Once I imagined "The King" giving me head but it wasn't nearly as sweet as when I'd think about you. (*Grins.*) No, in those moments, all the times when I'd close my eyes as you'd be *slurping* away down there, on my cock—I've never felt anything like that.

VELVET Gee, that makes me feel like a *hundred* bucks.

FRED It's a joke! The "Elvis" part, I mean.

VELVET Still . . .

FRED Come on, seriously! Where'd the name come from? Is it one of those things I already mentioned, or your ass or, or . . .

VELVET It's what I was wearing the first time a guy fucked me. At *nine*. I was raped in a dress I wore to church. With velvet bows on it. I was walking home with friends, my sister's friends who kept getting up there ahead of me and finally I was all alone. And, ummm . . . this man came by, in a truck and he . . . he said that he'd drive me back but he didn't. He did not. I was found by my daddy the next day, clutching one of those bows in my little . . . (*Cries.*) Anyway, that's where it came from. When I thought about that story and the dress . . . I started using that name for myself. So. (*Beat.*) Anyway. Still like it? "Velvet."

FRED Ummm . . . not as much. No.

VELVET Well, then.

FRED Jesus, that's . . . I'm . . .

VELVET Now you know.

FRED Really? (*Beat.*) I mean, is that—honestly?

VELVET Ha! (*Laughs.*) God, no! Please! You think I'd actually tell you something *personal* about me? Fat fucking chance.

FRED You bitch! That's awful . . .

VELVET Which part? The story or the fact that it didn't happen?

FRED . . . both . . .

VELVET Yeah, well, don't worry. It's happened to somebody before, just not me. At least in that way . . . (*Checks watch.*) Gotta go.

FRED So you can't put this person off just for today? You've got a guest here . . .

She goes into another part of the apartment to change her clothes. He follows her and they continue talking.

VELVET "Guest" I knew nothing about.

FRED Doesn't matter. I'm here now.

VELVET I can't.

FRED Wait! Come on . . .

VELVET Fred, I really can't. I gave my word . . .

FRED Oh shit, oh. I didn't realize it was *that* serious. Your "word."

VELVET I don't care what you think, that's very important to me. If I do that. It may not be a big thing to you, your line of work—

I'm not saying anything about what you do but lawyers are very—
nothing. It doesn't matter. I made a promise and that's that.

FRED What're you, like some Indian chief? Who the hell even talks
like that any more? "I gave my word." That's ridiculous. I'm not
judging you but you sound like some *retard* making statements
of that nature. Come on, just blow it off . . .

VELVET I said "I can't." I don't want to so I can't. Now please
move . . .

FRED Oh. I'm sorry. Lemme get outta here then so you can go have
espresso with some guy or whomever. Some man who's probably
this married dude who'll be telling his spouse that he's gotta run
back to the office on a Sunday—"I know, it's nutty!"—or take the
dog for an extra long walk since it's "so beautiful out!" Which one
is it? Hmm? Today, I mean, since I'm sure your roster is pretty
goddamn full. So which? (*Beat.*) I don't really buy the whole
"shopping and maybe some friends" business you're putting out
there so you might as well just be honest with me . . . go ahead.
Go. (*Beat.*) You may very well be . . . *yearning* to change who you
are or whatever but ya still gotta eat. So which one is it? Come
on! *Which*?!

*She finishes dressing and pushes out past him, back into the other
room. He follows her out.*

VELVET It's, ummmm . . . the "dog" one. Good guess.

FRED God, you make me sick . . .

VELVET Sorry. (*Beat.*) Anyway, I'm just saying what you wanna hear,
so whatever.

FRED No, not whatever! Anyway, it's you, so I shouldn't be very surprised.

VELVET No?

FRED Not very.

VELVET Well, forgive me for being so pedestrian about my affairs. My comings-and-goings.

FRED I don't believe that. That you feel at all that way . . . *contrite*.

VELVET Oh shit—what now? WHAT? (*Beat*.) You can't even let a person say they're sorry anymore without jumping on it or *challenging* every fucking word! You are exhausting! You really— what's the problem *now*? Hmm?

FRED That. The idea that you're not even one tiny bit sorry about what you do. Or who you do it with. Any of it.

VELVET Fred, ya know what? You're about a minute from being offi-cially "not welcome" here. Seriously. Sixty seconds from it.

FRED That sounds like a threat.

VELVET Not really. How could I threaten you? Big guy like you, here in my house—how would I be able to do that?

FRED You could throw something, I guess. That usually does it. Scares people. (*Grabs a ceramic candlestick holder and tosses it across the room. Smash!*) I bought 'em for you so I don't feel so bad. But hey, what good is one, right? (*He breaks the other one. Smash!*) You could do that. Or call the cops, maybe . . .

VELVET . . . that's . . . not good for anybody . . .

FRED Certainly not for you. With all the cash you've no doubt got stashed around your pad here. Unearned pay. Well, not that, "unearned," because you did do shit for it—shit that would probably make even Mae West blush and that chick supposedly did every-body in Hollywood . . . *every*-body! Even some of the ladies—but not "earned" income in the sense of tax returns and W-9's and a few things like that. Right? Am I right about *that* or not? Sweetie?

VELVET You're so fulla shit sometimes . . .

FRED Or my kid. You could call Chris and have him come over—lie to Mandy and run over here and have 'em try to kick my ass. He has a dog so he's even got a cover story ready, which no doubt you're aware of . . . and it certainly carries deep historical implications, as well—'s very classical. The son slaying the father. Anyway, I'm sure he wouldn't mind it, beating me up, drawing blood. Ol' Chris. Or giving it a try at least. Not so certain he could do it but hey, he's young and I'm getting older day by f-ing day. So maybe . . .

VELVET Or I could just ask you nice. And I will. (*Beat.*) Fred, it's good to see you again, even if you don't believe me it's true . . . I'm glad and maybe we can even do lunch or . . . some other . . .

FRED "Lunch!" Good one! Yeah, let's *eat* . . .

VELVET Fuck you!

FRED Exactly. I mean that's sorta the point of all this, in the end, isn't it? Me and my wanting to fuck you. Again.

VELVET I'm serious! Fuck. You. Fred. Goddamnit! I mean, I am trying to be some sort of civil person here and you're . . . just . . .

FRED I know, I know, and that's very—but come on! "Lunch!" That's a joke with you, you meeting guys for lunch. Isn't it? Isn't that just, like, a code word for their little desk thingies there, calendars? "Lunch with V. 2pm. Thurs." Please! You want "lunch?" Come on. Treat me with a little bit of respect . . .

VELVET Whatever.

FRED No, not whatever—I don't like the way you guys, kids now, say that and it fits anything they want it to, allows them to blow off all things painful or troubling or difficult. "Whatever." No, not that . . . No! Just *answer* me. Do you really mean I would meet you for lunch and sit with you and eat a salad or something . . . or is that a word that means other things when you use it? Things that would cost me about 500 bucks. Or so . . . (*Beat.*) I really am curious.

She is about to respond but stops herself—she waits for a beat, then speaks flatly. Honestly.

VELVET You haven't changed very much . . . (*Beat.*) Actually I can get anywhere up to about, I dunno, 700 dollars these days, and so yes . . . it's sometimes used that way. By me . . . "Lunch." But you know what? Not always. Some days it really does mean a slice of pizza and laughs with one of my pals—I do have a certain number of people in my life who I'd consider just that: "pals," believe it or not—surprising, huh? Well hey, I'm complex. What can I say?

FRED Huh. And Chris? What do you guys call it—"lunch" or something else? I'm curious.

VELVET That's different. He's special.

FRED I *bet.*

VELVET He is! He actually is a very special . . . why am I even trying to make you get it? Hmmm? It doesn't matter if you—Chris is very close to my heart and he's now one of my dearest friends. Someone I'm able to talk to and share my feelings with . . . yes, my actual dreams and all that shit! He even helped me get into art school . . . bet you didn't know that. Did you?

FRED . . . no. I didn't. (*Beat.*) He *and* Mandy or was it just him?

VELVET You're such a bastard, Fred, really! It's kind of breathtaking . . .

FRED Yeah, but it's also nothing new. So . . .

VELVET That's true enough.

FRED I just don't wanna put my boy up on some pedestal quite yet, not until I have all the facts about his *philanthropy* . . . that would be kinda pre-mature, even for his daddy. (*Beat.*) So books and parking, too, or just the tuition?

VELVET He encouraged my photography—he doesn't *pay* for it, if that's what you mean.

FRED I don't mean a thing. I'm just *giddy* with curiosity. That's all.

VELVET I'll bet.

FRED You can count on it. I promise.

VELVET You know what? It's now getting late. You should go.

FRED I should, shouldn't I?

VELVET Yes. Please.

FRED Well, I mean, if you're gonna say *please* then I have no recourse . . .

VELVET For what?

FRED To leave. You don't want me here, then I better go.

VELVET Look, I don't mean to be so . . . but . . .

FRED No, really, I get it! You got more to do on your day off than listen to me go on and on about nothing—you've got "lunch" to get to. A 700 dollar lunch.

VELVET You prick.

FRED That sounds delicious . . .

VELVET Just leave, ok? Don't make me get all . . .

FRED What?

VELVET *What?*

FRED I'm saying what does that mean? What's the next line when you say that—it makes me laugh when people do stuff like that! They do it and have nothing behind it.

VELVET What're you talking about? I just asked you to . . . you know . . . to get out.

FRED Yeah, you threatened me—let's call it what it is, a threat— with your little "don't make me . . ." but then what? Hmm? Are you gonna hit me? I don't think so. Break things, like I do? That's not like you. Too low-class. And I feel pretty sure you're not gonna call the police, like you said earlier, that's no good here and you're not gonna get my terrific and handsome son to

come over and do the dirty work for you so, really, it makes me
very curious: what the fuck are you gonna do if I just stay put?
Huh? (*Beat.*) I'm sorry to use bad language like that, you know
that's not who I really am but sometimes a word like that . . .
it just has no equivalent. It's the perfect word for the moment
and once in a while "fuck" is that word. So I will ask you again
. . . what the *fuck* will you do if I decide to camp out here?
Hmmm? What?

VELVET Fred . . . just . . . please go.

FRED I know, I hear you saying that, but I'm asking what happens
next? If I decide to not honor that request?

VELVET Ok, this is just getting . . . I mean . . . shit! Why does this
have to be . . . ? (*She faces him.*) This is what I'll do. If you stay.
Ummmmmmm . . . I'm gonna go into my bedroom and lock the
door and put on my make-up and hope you come back to your
goddamn senses—I'm sorry that you've left your wife, ok? I'm
sorry! And I can tell you are in pain but that's—so I'll do that, get
ready, and pray you've gone from my house when I come out.
(*Beat.*) That's all I've got, Fred. *That's* my backup plan.

FRED Ok. Got it.

VELVET Yep.

FRED Well, at least it's something . . .

VELVET Fred.

FRED I mean, it's not much but hey, it's at the very least a plan.
Your little plan. (*Beat.*) Just so you know, though . . . that wouldn't
stop me.

VELVET Please don't say stuff like that . . .

FRED I'm not saying I'm going to attack you! Stop! Jesus, don't make this so dramatic. I'm not saying that. To you. (*Beat.*) I'm saying that a bedroom door—I've put in a few in my day, our lake house or places like that—and they're mostly hollow-core doors. Like *egg cartons* inside and I'd be able to kick and punch my way through it in about five minutes. Tops. Just so you don't start feeling all safe and secure in there just because you push that tiny little button on the handle—you're just dreaming if you think that means you're okay. If I wanted to get at you, I mean.

VELVET Fine. Then I'll just leave it open and hope you snap outta this and go . . .

FRED You really want me outta here *that* bad? I've only been here half an hour, so I must've really—do you? Want me gone?

VELVET I do now, yes.

FRED Ok. But not when you first saw me?

VELVET No, ummm, no, but . . . now . . . yes. Please.

FRED No, I mean when you opened the door, when I was out there in your hallway and I'm carrying all of these stupid *satchels* and Samsonites—you're telling me that inside your heart didn't drop a little and you thought to yourself, "ohh shit, what is Fred doing here?" The truth now . . .

VELVET No, Fred, it wasn't like that.

FRED Really?

VELVET It was a surprise. Like I said.

FRED A *nice* surprise?

VELVET Yes! I guess so. Please, I'm not . . . it was *surprising*. That was my first—it caught me off-guard, that's what happened. That was my very first reaction. "Surprise."

FRED Yeah?

VELVET Yes. Not anger. Not feeling sick. It was nice to see your face again but yes, it's very surprising for you to be here. With me. Like this.

FRED I agree.

VELVET Ok.

FRED I totally agree with that.

VELVET Thank you. Thanks.

FRED But that's what I love about it, too. The surprise of it. The honesty. I love that!

VELVET Do you?

FRED Absolutely! You're seeing me naked. For maybe the first time in my life—or since you've known me, anyway—you're seeing me stand up in front of you, the lights are on and I'm not covering myself as I slip into the bathroom but standing there so you can see who I am. This is *me*. A man who's now for once in his life free from all the other junk that's been holding me back for so so long. (*Beat.*) I came right here to you . . . straight here so I could show you what I really look like as a man unburdened of a lifetime of shit . . . the responsibilities that I took on and suffered through and dragged myself back to the office because of. I'm right here. Only now are you seeing me as I really am—this is the "Fred" I've always wanted to show you! Begged to show you. *This* guy.

VELVET And I appreciate that. I do, but . . .

FRED No, really, I don't think you get it. I am now the real me here. *Me!*

VELVET No, Fred, I can see that you're . . .

FRED Finally! (*Grabs her by the shoulders.*) For the first time ever with you I'm able to show you that boy I was growing up, this kid who had dreams and, and wanted to be loved and to love in return—I sound like a bad TV movie but you know I'm serious! Being truthful. This is *me*, and I ran to you after I walked out on Miriam to show you this guy. To see if there was still some way that we could . . . you know. Make this happen. That probably sounds a bit foolish but that's how you still make me feel, just the *memory* of you. It is.

VELVET Ummmm . . . but it's been, like, four years now.

FRED No, I know!

VELVET Ok, then. Just so you do.

FRED But that's . . . I mean, people still . . .

VELVET Yes! People do funny things. They see an old friend from high school after three decades and they realize that's the man they've been secretly in love with all of their life. I'm aware that it happens. Or after being in a war or, or some relative who you've got no business feeling like that about . . . love's *insane* sometimes! I get that, I do.

FRED See? I knew you would. We're so . . . ! (*Beat.*) Remember when Chris brought you out to our lake house? That one summer? The bar-b-que was going and I'm at the grill, grinning like an asshole while I'm making small talk with you and Chris is in talking to his mom and then you . . . you just dropped your whole . . . whatever it was . . . skirt or, or, dress-thingie. You just dropped it. Down around your feet . . . like it was the most natural thing in the world. And as you're going down to pick it up . . . bending over there at the waist to retrieve it, you glanced over at me . . . looked me square in the eye with a tiny little smile as you scooped it up and then ran off in your little bikini there into the house. To find my son. (*Beat.*) I burned the shit outta the burgers, I remember that! But from that moment on . . . I mean, from that very *second* . . . I knew I had to be with you, no matter what. That there was no one more beautiful or important or worth being with in this whole world than you. No one . . . (*Beat.*) I'm sure that probably sounds stupid but that's what this stirs up again . . . me just being here with you after all this time. I feel free to get down on one knee and say what I've felt for so long. To remind you how much I've always loved you.

VELVET But—oh God, why're you doing this to me today?—I don't feel that, Fred. Not for you. I *don't*. (*Beat.*) Look at you now, the way you're glaring at me, but I'm trying to be honest, so . . . I just don't love you. Not like that. Not any more.

FRED Oh. (*Beat.*) You don't.

VELVET No.

FRED I see.

VELVET I'm sorry, but it's . . . how *could* I? It's been so long and we've . . . how would that even be possible right now? Really?

FRED No, I mean, if that's how you feel about me then I don't want you trying to be . . .

VELVET I am sorry.

FRED Yeah, you said that. "Sorry." It wasn't so great the first time and now it just sounds repetitive, so maybe come up with something else . . . ok?

VELVET Please don't be mean right now.

FRED I can't really help it! I just threw away my other life for you. FOR YOU.

VELVET But that's . . . I didn't ask you to . . .

FRED I know you didn't ask me to. Ok, ok, ok! I'm aware of that little fact, that crack in my fucking plan or *armor* or whichever of those gets cracks in them! OK. I did it all on my own and now I'm . . . I . . . but I thought it would *matter* at least! To you. That I did what I said I'd do after all those other times. That I finally did the thing should at least mean something . . . All the way here on the plane, I believed that you were at *least* gonna respond to that. The pure gesture of it. What I did.

VELVET It's . . . Fred, it's very flattering, but . . .

FRED I'm not a *toddler*, alright? Don't be some condescending bitch to me right now! This is not turning out to be a great day for me . . . this is a self-image killer and I'm not gonna make it through if that's how you handle this. "Flattering!" Fuck that. I just pissed away the rest of my life to be with you—sorry I didn't phone first!—but that's the truth of it. Right there.

VELVET Okay, ummm . . . lemme just think for a . . .

FRED God, you'd love a SWAT team to come bashing through that door right about now, wouldn't you? Huh? *Huh*?!

VELVET Stop.

FRED Ha! (*Laughing.*) I can't stop! I don't know if you've been listening to me very close for the last little while but this shit's just *bubbling* outta me right now and I'm not exactly in control so, you know . . . hold on to your hats! Or whatever they say. Who says crap like that? Cowboys? Not the football team, I don't mean them but the other guys. The wild west ones—do they say it?

VELVET I'm not sure.

FRED Huh. Well, you don't know too much about anything right now, do ya? Doesn't seem like it to me. I mean, not anymore.

VELVET Not right now I don't. No.

FRED No?

VELVET Nope. I feel frozen and, and, and like I don't know about anything. Nothing.

FRED You're just trying to . . . whatever the hell they call it in the movies . . . you're just *placating* me right now. Aren't you?

VELVET . . . I don't even know what that means . . .

FRED Doesn't mean you don't know how to do it! Because you do. You do it, every time you open your big fucking mouth. So . . . (*Beat.*) Speaking of mouths I should watch it, my own, I mean, or wash it out with soap . . . listen to me! Swearing and all that, like I'm some horny teenager all pissed off . . .

She has begun to edge her way over to the bedroom door.

VELVET Fred, I need to—look, I have to make a call. I'm now close to being late.

FRED He'll wait. Who wouldn't, for you? He'll order an *appetizer*, don't worry . . .

VELVET That's not the point, ok? I need to call. It's the right thing to do . . .

FRED Yeah? Is that how it's done now? A *call?*

VELVET Yes. It is. And if it was you I'd do the same thing . . .

FRED Oh, man, thanks, baby . . . thank you so *so* much! (*Beat.*) You know, it's true what they say about you guys: you really do have hearts of gold . . .

VELVET Fred! Fuck, just stop it!! STOP!! I mean, shit . . . you're getting . . . *so* . . .

FRED What? Seriously, I'd love to know what I am to you. Right now.

VELVET Nuts about this! I'm sorry but you are!!

FRED Sweetie, you don't know the half of it . . .

VELVET So then, maybe that's the answer. Right? You've finally gone bonkers and there's not anything I can say to help you or, or stop you or whatever—maybe you just went schizo like you always warned me you were gonna do . . . maybe that's it.

FRED Could be. I am feeling a little unhinged right now, so . . . who knows? (*Beat.*) I mean, you should've seen me walking over here from the, whatchamacallit, the train. Or subway-thingie. I couldn't get a cab so I took that in from the airport and all the way here and even on the street, I think I was talking to myself. I was. Mumbling shit and holding all that crap over there on the floor. I must've been a sight! Can you imagine, middle-aged guy, dressed in a fancy suit and *blubbering* to himself?

VELVET I'm sorry about that, I really am but . . . I mean, what do you want me to do here, Fred? Seriously. *What*?

FRED Ultimately? Suck my cock, but I'm willing to sweet-talk ya a little bit more first.

VELVET Gee, thanks.

FRED No, thank you! Thanks for being so good at your job and so goddamn understanding! (*Beat.*) I know that sounds like me being a real asshole, but you always wanted the truth being used—at least on paper—so there it is. You're *great* at what you do.

VELVET What's that?

FRED Whatever we guys want you to do. Or gals, too, probably. I'm sure you don't sniff at the cash if it comes from some lady, either, do you? You're very progressive like that . . . (*Beat.*) I bet there's some video footage of that somewhere that me and Chris could jack off to for hours!

VELVET You know what? I really am going in the other room now, so you do . . . whatever it is you wanna do . . .

She tries to slip inside and shut the door but he gets there first. They struggle a bit. He pulls her to him.

She backs away and tries to defuse the situation. Takes a few steps back into the other room as he follows her.

FRED No, don't go. Come on! (*Stops her.*) Don't run off, just . . . !

VELVET Fred, please . . . don't get in front of me like that! Don't!

FRED What, why can't I? Why shouldn't I get in your way, make things hard for you—name me one good reason! Hmmm!

VELVET Fred, stop it!

FRED Just stay here! I wanna talk to you! You don't need to go running off when I'm . . .

VELVET Stop this!!

FRED Then sit down! Sit down so we can talk or I'm gonna . . . !

VELVET What?! You'll what?!!

FRED Just . . . don't push me, ok? I don't need to be *pushed* at all today! I'm serious now!

VELVET Okay! Fine, I'll sit. But I have to make that call . . .

FRED Go, then! Fuck, do what you gotta do! But then I wanna finish this and if we—then I'll go. I promise. I'll pick up my shit and wander off and you can go find your fucking *soul* or . . . whatever it is you're searching for. (*Beat.*) Who knows? Maybe you'll find out that you don't have one! That's why I never look at myself. For that very reason . . .

VELVET Ok, that's—can I call now?

FRED Yes. Please. It's your own home. (*Beat.*) But from in here, ok? Don't go sneaking off to the—call him from here.

VELVET But I really have to . . . I'm . . .

FRED Just *listen* and *do*, please. Ok? I'm your guest so do what I say. Call from here.

VELVET . . . fine. If that's what you—then you'll have to listen. Sorry, but that's up to you.

FRED Go ahead. I'm all ears.

VELVET Ok.

FRED Put on your sexy voice and get to it.

VELVET Shit. Fine. (*Picks up phone and dials.*) Hi there. It's me. Yeah, no, I'm calling now because I'm running a little—I'll be a bit later than I said. Is that ok? Will it be—do they still serve lunch at that point or . . . when does the kitchen close?

FRED Ha! (*To self.*) "Lunch."

VELVET What? Nothing, no . . . it's the TV. Yes, I'm sorry. Lemme turn it down. (*Beat.*) Anyway, let's still meet there and if we're late then

we'll find another spot. It's a city so there's lots of—exactly!
(*Laughs.*) We can do whatever we want. That's so true. Yeah,
I can't wait, either. No, I know . . . that's fine, we can talk about
that all you want, you know I'm ok with that. I really am! Good.
I'll see you there. And you, too. Ok. Yes. Alright. Bye, Chris.
(*She hangs up.*)

FRED . . . no, no, no. Don't tell me that was . . . not *my* Chris . . .
that'd be . . . because the coincidence would be just *too* delicious!

VELVET Yeah.

FRED Seriously, who was that?

VELVET It was Chris. Now can we . . . ?

FRED Yeah, but there must be a million guys in this town named
that. And girls, too . . . it's really such a crap name, so common.
Sorry I ever named my son that. "Chris."

VELVET Fred, it was *Chris*. I'm seeing him later today. Supposed to
be there in an hour . . .

FRED Well, you better get to it, then. Fuck, I do not wanna mess
up a quaint little get-together like that! (*Gets up and goes to his
bags.*) Just help me get all this . . .

VELVET You asked me to call from here! I didn't want to! So . . .

FRED Yeah, well, maybe you should've pleaded a little harder!
You know?! For my sake!

VELVET Come on, that's bullshit! Seriously! You bullied me into
doing it right in front of you and now you'ro all . . . don't act so
hurt just because I'm . . . I'm . . .

FRED I mean, what're the odds, huh?! I'd leave his mom today and
come here, to see you, and you're running out the door to meet
up with *him*! That's like some, I dunno . . . one of those fucking
Neil Simon plays or something. That's just *not* possible . . .

VELVET I'm sorry.

FRED No, don't be.

VELVET Fred . . .

FRED It's very sobering, actually. Woke me up, just like that. (*Beat.*)
You've broken the spell, so thank you . . .

He takes a little bow and moves over to his pile of bags.

VELVET What? (*Beat.*) Look, once you're settled, maybe we can, you
know . . . maybe . . .

FRED Ha! Another one.

VELVET What?

FRED Another of those shit half-sentences that you really have no
intention of finishing and hope that I don't call you on.

VELVET No, it isn't.

FRED Bullshit! Ok, go on, then. Once I get a motel somewhere
and I've got all my stuff put away, *socks* in a drawer, then what?
I should be expecting your call? Perhaps meet for "lunch?"
Gimme a fucking . . . !

VELVET I didn't say that! But we can *talk* more about this . . .
something like that. Ok? We can, just not right now . . . when I'm . . .

FRED . . . when you're about to go get my son's cock up your ass. Yeah, that is bad timing . . .

VELVET Jesus Christ, stop it! Stop being so . . . my God, you're just being horrible right now. *Horrible.* Why? What did I do to you?

FRED Do you really want me to answer that?

VELVET I do, yeah. Even if I'm late I want to hear your side of that. *What*, Fred? To make you say such nasty shit to me . . .

FRED Ok. Lemme see . . . (*Beat.*) I suppose I'd start with . . . maybe . . . I dunno. I'm not that sure anymore. I just know I hate you . . . I mean, if I can't have you then that's all I've got left. Is this *rage* inside at not being the one you'd pick.

VELVET Where is that fair?! I mean, to another person? Huh?!

FRED Who said anything about fair? Are you at all listening to me?! I'm talking about love here, ok? LOVE. When has that shit ever been about being *fair*?

VELVET I guess that's true enough. (*Beat.*) And so those're the only two possibilities?! Me and you, together forever, or you despise me for *eternity*? Nothing in between?

FRED Pretty much.

VELVET Well, that's great . . .

FRED Isn't that the usual course it takes? I'm not a fortune teller but I listen pretty good in court and that's the story I keep hearing, time and time again. It's love or hate. That's all there is, really . . .

VELVET Well, not for me. Sorry, but I don't . . .

FRED No?

VELVET Not at all. No.

FRED Then enlighten me. Seriously. Tell me all the good news you've found out during the soul-searching you've been doing—fill up my heart and open my eyes. (*Beat.*) Please, go on. I'm all ears . . .

VELVET Yeah, you'll think it's crap, I'm sure, but I do believe in the middle. The in-between. That we can find many degrees of happiness and, and *love* and the opposite, too, variations of hate that aren't just the same old anger and destruction . . . I'm sure of it now, after years of . . . you're standing there with a smirk on your face so think whatever. I don't care. I don't love you, Fred, it's not possible right now, but I certainly don't hate you or want to punish you or anything close to that . . . I think with time we might even find our way to . . . I dunno, some lovely place! I think it's possible. But not right now . . . not this *minute*. (*Beat.*) We both have some other stuff to deal with first. Ok? Don't we?

FRED Yeah, no . . . I get that. (*Beat.*) I might not like admitting it but yes, it makes some kinda sense.

VELVET Good.

FRED It does.

VELVET Thank you.

FRED I thought you were just gonna spout a lot of stupid Middle Eastern shit but . . . that actually . . . you make some good sense.

VELVET That's . . . I'm glad. And we can talk more about it when we've . . . you know . . .

FRED When?

VELVET I don't know, but sometime in the near . . .

FRED No, I mean *when* like let's set a date. If that's what I need to do with you, get an appointment, then I'd rather just do that and have one and I'll know where I stand.

VELVET . . . ok, but we don't have to do that right now . . .

FRED No, it's easier. For me. (*Beat.*) Tuesday?

VELVET Fred, please . . .

FRED If that's bad, I can do Wednesday.

VELVET I have class then.

FRED I left out Monday. How's Monday?

VELVET Bad. Sorry. I can't. I have a "thing."

FRED 'Kay. God, busy bee, aren't ya? So if not then, when? You tell me.

VELVET Ummmm . . . next weekend is pretty ok.

FRED Really? *Squeeze* me in on Saturday, maybe?

VELVET I was thinking Sunday, but . . . that's . . .

FRED Ha! Are you kidding me or not?

VELVET No.

FRED Seriously? Not Saturday but *Sunday*?

VELVET If that's ok with you.

FRED Yeah, it's great! I'm here for you! To see you and, and,
I dunno, I hoped be near you in some way but if I've got to jockey
for a spot with your yoga class then maybe I'll just jump on the
shuttle back to Maryland and wait for your call! Maybe I should
do that! Huh?

VELVET . . . maybe you should.

FRED Excuse me?

VELVET Nothing.

FRED No, go ahead. Say it.

VELVET It's none of my business . . . so no.

FRED Doesn't matter. Say it to me.

VELVET I think you probably should do that. Go back home and
think about this—call me on the phone and we'll talk and see
what is what but we won't have to have this . . . some big scene in
my living room.

FRED You think *this* is big . . . what we've been doing here? Do ya?

VELVET Kinda. Yeah, I do.

FRED Then you've got a shit memory.

VELVET Why's that? Because of how we finished?

FRED Exactly.

VELVET I haven't forgotten, don't worry.

FRED Well, that's good. Something positive did come out of it, just like you promised . . .

VELVET Fred, I'm just saying . . .

He waves her off, heading over to a couch. He plops down.

FRED Don't bother. I don't like most of the trash that spills outta your mouth now . . . not even twenty percent of it. If you were a baseball player you'd be laughed outta the fucking game, the number of times you do something worth noting. *Humiliated* and laughed right off the fucking field!

VELVET Why're you so mad at me, Fred? So *bitter*? I didn't do anything here. Nothing.

FRED So what? Shit happens to people all the time, outta the blue. Doesn't matter. It is all about how we deal with it, once it lands at our feet.

VELVET Is that right?

FRED Yes.

VELVET Really? I mean . . .

FRED Yep. That's the truth—the answer is *in* the struggle. That's where we shine or we roll over like little bitches and die in the dirt, with our guts exposed and flies shitting in our open mouths. (*Beat.*) Look, I'm not mad. Ok? I'm just very, very disappointed. Alright?

VELVET . . . I understand . . .

FRED No, I don't think you do or you'd take me in the other room and blow me, just outta sympathy for an old guy who's just tossed his life in the fucking river! That's the kind of thing you'd do if you understood.

VELVET Is that what you want? You want me to get on my knees and do that for you and make the whole world start spinning again?

FRED Tell you what—I wouldn't hate it.

VELVET Yeah?

FRED And then I'd go. I mean, for now. Not all the way back home, maybe, but somewhere. Maybe to Chris's house for a few days or something like that. (*Beat.*) Kidding.

VELVET . . . Chris isn't . . .

FRED What?

VELVET Nothing.

FRED No, not nothing. Don't say that . . .

VELVET Look, it's not for me to . . . to be . . .

FRED Just say it! I hate games. You know that about me. I hate little fucking games, so tell me. (*Beat.*) Stop grinning! You know a thing about Chris that I don't and you're feeling superior about it, so say it . . .

VELVET He's not living at home right now.

FRED What?

VELVET He and his—he's got his own place. Has now for a few months.

FRED He's not at—*months*? That's bullshit.

VELVET Call him up. Ask him.

FRED I'm asking *you* . . . what're you even . . . ?

VELVET I just told you and you said it's a lie so call him up if you can't believe me. Seriously, blow his mind with a random "hey, son, how ya doing?" Go on.

FRED What's that supposed to mean?

VELVET Not anything.

FRED Well, well . . . aren't you two just chummy? He's told ya all that, that I don't call him enough?

VELVET In so many words.

FRED What a fucking pussy. I'm sorry, he's my kid and some amazing computer guy but I think he's a little baby most times.

VELVET . . . imagine what he thinks of you.

FRED Please don't get smart with me, ok? This really is not the day for it . . .

VELVET Fine.

FRED Huh. Little fucker left his wife. Jesus, he even beat me to that! Good boy! He's spent his *whole* life trying to show me up at everything—did a pretty good job of it, too!—and now he's trumped the ol' man on that one as well. I'll be a son-of-a-bitch . . .

VELVET Yeah, so . . . do it. Call him if you don't believe me.

FRED No, that's alright. I do. I believe you. Why else would you
say it?

VELVET I wouldn't.

FRED Yeah, that much I do believe. You'd never just say it for effect.
Not you.

VELVET Nope.

FRED That's not like you . . . you like the truth better. That's the shit
that *really* hurts a person. The cold hard truth.

VELVET Wow. I mean . . . do you hate *every*-body or is it just me?

FRED Most . . . but you're special. (*Beat.*) I hate you in a special way.

VELVET Nice.

FRED Hey, I thought you were into the "truth."

VELVET I am, it's just kinda . . . shocking to hear.

FRED Yeah, well, it goes both ways. And it's not how I was feeling
two hours ago . . . you had to really *grind* my ego into the carpet
first before I got to that place.

VELVET Don't say that.

FRED Why not? It's true, ever since I got here it's been one long
shove to get me back out the door. I'm sorry that I've made a
mess of your day, your little trip to the zoo with my son! I am
terribly sorry for having spent the last couple years wanting you,
pining for your touch. I am so, so very sorry that I fell in love with

you back when you seemed like somebody who felt the same about me! You didn't, obviously, you never did but I sure as shit believed it there for a while. You made me a goddamn believer in all things being possible, and I can't help it or feel bad about it or sorry. Falling in love at my age, you think I'm gonna be able to regret that? Not on your life.

VELVET I don't regret it either, Fred. I never have . . . any feelings I've had for you.

FRED Yeah?

VELVET Not one day. Not even the day you left, which was sorta mind-blowing in its . . . explosiveness . . . but even then I didn't hate anything that ever happened between us. (*Beat.*) If you don't think I was in love with you at one point then you just weren't listening . . .

FRED Maybe so.

VELVET Absolutely so! (*Beat.*) There was a moment there where I would've run off to *China* with you on a dogsled . . . that's dumb but you know what I mean . . . anything. I was ready to do *any*-thing with you or for you or, or . . . all of it. I was yours . . . (*Beat.*) I stopped asking for money and we spent some of the most . . . I dunno, *moving* days of my life together. In bed. On various trips and, and . . . you know that's true. You make whatever faces you want to now but inside you know it . . . I loved you.

FRED No, I . . . fuck. I know that. I'm . . . yes. I do know. At least for a second there. I *had* you. Didn't I?

VELVET You really did. Completely. I broke it off with your son,
I crushed him and he never really forgave me—yes, we see each
other now and he's begun to trust me some but there's still a
little dark spot when he looks at me, in his eyes—but I did it for
you. To be with you. And all I asked was for some time, time to
let the smoke clear and for me to . . . not even selfishly, not just
for me, but so that Chris wasn't just absolutely *squashed* in the
wreckage. Just so I didn't have to face that, too, on top of the
rest. I knew what he was gonna say, once he found out about us
. . . what could he say? Nothing good. And I knew what it meant,
you leaving home and taking up with me, what you were facing
but we wanted it, wanted to be with each other so bad, to keep
that tiny spark of whatever you'd call it that we ignited in each
other—but I just asked you for a few weeks. *Weeks!* And you
couldn't do it.

FRED . . . no . . . that's not . . .

VELVET I'm talking now, Fred, alright? *I* am. I listened to a bunch
of your shit here, in my home when I'm supposed to be going
out the door to see a friend of mine—I have stayed and taken
in all of the *bile* and mean-spirited crap you've tossed at me
because I don't love you this minute so you can hear me out
now. What I have to say. (*Beat.*) I needed to back off a bit.
Yes . . . I asked for us to turn it down a notch and take a deep
breath, sleep in our own beds for a few nights just so it didn't
feel like we were covered in blood but you couldn't do it. The
more I pulled back the tighter you put your hand around my
throat. I couldn't wake up without the feeling of your fingers,
digging into my neck—calling me and the texts . . . I mean,
like, hundreds of texts! *Daily.* And if I was out or couldn't call

back then your messages got darker and meaner until finally—
that's what you gave me when I was really in need of you.
Of you understanding me.

FRED It was a bad time for me, too! Come on. That's not . . .
completely . . .

VELVET I know that! I just said all that, and I can imagine what it feels
like, to go so so far with a person and then have a plug pulled on
you, even for a few days, I can sympathize with you and, I dunno,
maybe I even went about it the wrong way but I'm telling you now
like I did back then, it was *vital* to me. After all that I'd been put
through with your son and you and my school stuff . . . (*Beat.*)
I never would've asked if it wasn't an emergency. And so what'd
you do? You came into my hospital bed and fucked the shit outta
me, every night. Without fail. Metaphorically, or course, but it felt
like it all the same. When what I needed was for you to just . . .
hold me, to put your arms around me tight and hug me and tell me
I could have all the time in the world if I wanted it . . . you turned
me over and just kept sticking your dick in me. Day after day after
day. Until I couldn't take it any more . . .

FRED Huh. Okay. If that's how you—I mean, it seems like a little bit
of revisionist . . . history or whatever, but fine. If that's your story,
stick with it. (*Beat.*) I'm a little confused, though. You said "night"
and then it was "day" and then—so which was it? Hmmmm? Get
the facts straight if you're gonna *hurl* shit like that right in my face.
When was I metaphorically doing you again in which metaphorical
hospital? At what *metaphorical* time? Please, help me out here,
'cause . . . I'm a little . . .

He gets in her face now, pinning her up against one wall.

VELVET   Just forget it.

FRED   No, really, I'm trying to grasp the . . .

VELVET   You don't see it that way? What happened between us?

FRED   Ummmm, no. I really don't.

VELVET   Fine, then. (*Beat.*) Fine.

FRED   Yeah, let's leave it where it is. Dead.

VELVET   That's ok by me.

FRED   Sure, now that you got to throw that ball of shit in my face, absolutely. *Now* let's drop it.

VELVET   That wasn't the point. To rub your face in it. I was *trying* to be . . .

FRED   And yet here I am—covered in shit all the same. (*Beat.*) After all I did for you!

VELVET   Yeah, "all" but never enough. Never anything real or genuine . . . just these . . .

FRED   . . . fucking *gifts*, and, and, and . . . !

VELVET   No! That's not, no . . . they were never just that! Gifts. They were *tests* and traps or ways to control me . . . to see how I'd react or *if* I'd react—that's what you gave me! Little prizes if I loved you enough . . .

FRED   Ha! Yeah, that sounds about right! Un-*fucking*-grateful. I gave you everything!

He lets her go and walks away. Instead of retreating, she follows him around and keeps on about the subject.

VELVET No, that's not even—you know that is not true! I don't care what else you say here but you know I was grateful. But you're—everything means *every*-thing. Not *lots* of things, or *some* things. Not just what you wanna give. It means all you've got. *All.*

FRED That's so . . . I can't even understand you! And I don't care what you say, all the rationalizing of what you were—it just stopped! WHAM! The way you felt toward me . . . I don't know what you were thinking on your side but from where I stood, it felt like a fucking door slamming in my face. BAM! Just like that. BAM!!

VELVET That's not true.

FRED The truth is subjective, sweetie. Always has been.

VELVET No, that isn't—what's true is true.

FRED You should read some more history books, then. (*Beat.*) Winners write those things, they get to scribble down shit and that's what we remember. They lived so what they get as a reward is "history." To rewrite history and that's what you're doing . . .

VELVET No. Stop! There were *lots* of things we . . .

FRED I'm just saying—one day you were all up in my face, kisses and *whispers* and that little smile of yours, we were all in it together . . . and then, BANG! Like you found out I was fucking your *sister*, I was held at arm's length and, and your calls start tapering off . . . God, it was like a . . .

VELVET . . . that's because of what I said . . . *that's* the shit I'm talking about! Choking me!

FRED Yeah, but it was more than that—even the way you looked at me! Something was gone.

VELVET No, that's not . . . it didn't happen like . . . you *forced* me to! I made a decision about us because of your pestering me!! It was you who started the whole . . . it was YOU!!

FRED Nobody wants to remember killing somebody so it's natural, but that's how it went. Trust me.

VELVET No, you pressured me! I just told you!! It was too much at that time, just right at that one time so I hit the brakes . . . that's all I did. I slowed us down . . .

FRED Not "slowed," stopped! Stopped us cold! WHAM! Just like that!

VELVET I had to!

FRED Nobody *has* to do anything! You *chose* to!!

VELVET That's not—no! I HAD TO! It had to end!

FRED Hey, whatever helps you sleep at night . . .

VELVET Stop it! STOP! I'm not gonna let you do that to me, not anymore or ever again!! I'm not here to *service* your fantasies or your anger at me now, your hatred—I will *not* be that person for you, so forget it! You couldn't pay me enough . . .

FRED I'm not sure that's true—everybody's got a price. Especially you, honey.

VELVET You fucking asshole! ASSHOLE! How can you even say shit like that to me? Huh? After all we've been—no. I will not engage you in this because that is what you want . . . you *want* me to be some ugly, twisted version of myself, denying you what you need but that's not what's happening. That is *not* what's really going on here today . . .

FRED Of course not. You'd never acknowledge who you really are and that's because you're selfish. SELF-ISH. (*Beat.*) All you've ever cared about is you . . .

VELVET That's bullshit and you know it! You know that, Fred!! This, right here, is why you hate games—because you can't stand it if you lose. Right? Isn't that true? (*Beat.*) And it's eating you up inside because the *truth* is I didn't really cast you aside like you wanna believe. No. *Fact* is you *lost* me. Minute by minute, with each of your questions and demands and all your petty little tantrums—you drove me away!! And it kills you inside to acknowledge that. The fucking truth.

FRED No, you just don't like the taste of blood in your mouth . . .

VELVET Fred, that's . . . I can't do this now!! I really should get going. (*Beat.*) I'll go without make-up . . . I'll just . . .

FRED My boy's not gonna like that. He likes a good, clean woman. I may not've been the model dad but I know my kid's taste. At least in the ladies. (*Beat.*) Actually, I think his tastes are a little suspect—I've always thought he might be kinda, ya know. Hetero-*flexible*. Ol' Chrissy.

VELVET Please don't be like this right— (*Beat.*) Don't destroy *every*-thing in your path. Me, I can take it but if you're mad at me don't take it out on your kid and, and, and the whole world and . . . please don't.

FRED Hey, baby, I'm here. If not now, when? I am at least as smart as you are and you know I'm never getting back through that door again, not without a police warrant so it's now or never. Correct?

VELVET . . . Fred . . .

FRED I mean, read *Lolita* sometime . . . this shit *always* ends badly.

VELVET Ha! You're still funny, Fred. I'm glad to see that.

FRED Yeah, I'm a real card.

VELVET No, you are . . . you know that's true. You can be a very funny person and it's one of the things that always attracted me toward you.

FRED Really?

VELVET Absolutely.

FRED And here I've been thinking it was my big thick cock all this time . . .

VELVET See? Even that's a little bit funny.

FRED Just a *touch*. And obviously not the case.

VELVET No. Not true. I like it just fine but . . .

FRED Probably better not to finish that answer or I'll never take my pants off again.

VELVET Ha! It's nice when you're being this way.

FRED Well, I'm trying. My stomach's in knots here but I am trying! "Ho-ho-ho."

VELVET I know you are and I appreciate it.

FRED No, I know you always liked the funny me or the light-hearted me . . . *that* guy. You made that pretty clear and that's who I always tried to be but sometimes it just seemed as if maybe you liked my wallet a lot more than any other part of me . . .

VELVET Fred, that's . . . that is actually a shit thing to say to me. After all we've been through.

FRED It's just a thought! Tell me I'm wrong.

VELVET You are wrong. Completely.

FRED Fine, then. I take it back.

VELVET Yeah?

FRED I do. Sorry I said it and I never really meant it . . . not actually.

VELVET . . . not sure I believe you, but . . .

FRED Well, you're gonna have to.

VELVET I don't *have* to do anything.

FRED That's true. Well, not completely. You *have* to meet Chris now . . . you "promised."

VELVET You know what I mean!

FRED I do. I'm just fucking with ya . . .

VELVET And you love that, don't you?

FRED In some fashion or another. Yes.

VELVET Ha! And you thought, what? That's how ya might win me back, by coming here and . . . and start pushing me around and breaking shit? Ask to move in with me *today*? Did you actually see that working out . . . in your head? Huh? I'm not being mean when I say this to you, but—was that *really* gonna happen in your fantasy?

FRED . . . yeah.

VELVET *Really?*

FRED I know that sounds—but yes. I thought maybe I could just *trot* right in here and plop down on the couch and be back in your loving embrace. Silly me.

VELVET I'm not saying that, calling you names, but that's sorta— I mean, you see that, right? In the light of day you can see where that's, like, just about a hundred percent impossible? (*Beat.*) And I'm saying today by that, not forever, not some date on the *Mayan* calendar but just this instant. I can't start in with you or up with you or anything even close to that *this* morning. It's impossible.

FRED Nothing's impossible—that's what you're gonna find out, at the end of your little spiritual journey, my dear. Anything is possible. *Any*-thing. And that's the only thing that keeps us from waking up and having our *Wheaties* and then blowing our fucking brains out. The tiny bit of hope I just offered you.

VELVET I'm not gonna argue with you.

FRED Don't have to. It's true. No sense in us arguing the truth . . .

VELVET Ok, cool then. Let's agree to disagree so we can—you do whatever but I have to get going now. I have my appointment.

FRED Fine.

VELVET I do. I wouldn't lie to you about it . . .

FRED No, I heard the call. I'm aware.

VELVET Alright then. (*Grabbing her stuff.*) You can, I dunno, take a bath or make some eggs before you go. If you want.

FRED Yeah? Should I leave a few bucks in the "honor jar" when I go—like a fucking bed & breakfast? (*Beat.*) Don't worry about me!

VELVET Fred . . . do whatever you want. I'm leaving.

FRED 'Kay. Say "hi" to "wonder boy" for me.

VELVET Stop calling him that!

FRED Please don't tell me anything about my son. That's really going *too* far if you do that . . .

VELVET No, seriously, *you* listen once! He hates that, he's told me so. Every since he was a kid and you started it after you saw a baseball movie. Some movie about—doesn't matter. You started in on him at his game once . . . some little league game that he struck out at and you began doing that. He knows you don't mean it and he really detests it when you call him that. So . . .

FRED "Detests" it? Really? His word or yours?

VELVET *His.* Underlined.

FRED Well, well . . . then I'll just have to stop, if that's the case. Wouldn't want my only child disliking something about me. That would just eat me up inside . . .

VELVET I don't think there's actually anything left inside you *to* eat up. But hey, just my opinion . . .

FRED Ha! Fucking touché, young lady. Touché!

VELVET You know where my extra key is. Just use it to lock the door. I gotta run.

FRED Alright. You go. (*Beat.*) Wait, just a sec' before you do, before you run off—why?

VELVET Why?

FRED Yeah, why?

VELVET Why *what*? Fred, please . . .

FRED No, I'm asking you so tell me. Go ahead. I can take it—why'd you do it? The first time?

VELVET Do—what? Stop. Come on.

FRED I just wanna know the truth! You like the truth so much . . . *love* it, you told me, so go on then, tell me all about it. Why'd you do what you did to me way back then? You might not even remember now . . . but I'm certainly curious.

VELVET Fred, I don't know what you're . . .

FRED The *note*. In my pocket. "GIRL FOR SALE." Why'd you do it?

VELVET No.

FRED "No?" What's that mean?

VELVET I'm not . . . no, I can't do that. Not right now. I'm fried, from this . . . what you've been doing here for the last—I'm not gonna go over a thing like that right now! I am not.

FRED Then call the cops . . . only way you'll ever get me outta here. But if *you* leave right now, at this moment? Then I will trash this place so bad you won't recognize it when you're coming back through that door. That's the god's-honest truth. I promise you. (*Beat.*) I'll burn this fucking *brothel* of yours to the ground if you walk out on me right now. *Velvet.*

VELVET Whatever you say, *Fred*. You've always had the cards on this . . . thing of ours . . . from the beginning. So go on then.

FRED Ha! It's "held," not "had."

VELVET What?

FRED When you're talking about cards. Just so when you use that *exact* line on the next idiot who stumbles in here with his pants around his ankles and a bundle of bags in his hands having left a wife and kids in his wake . . . next time you'll get it right. It's "*held* all the cards."

VELVET Whatever the fuck it is, you've always been the one, ok? "Holding" whatever.

FRED No, not even true! That's crap, total and false crap that you're—who *had* the cards when I found a little piece of stationery in my jacket? Hmmm? Asking me to "meet up in the city for a chat?" A fucking "chat" you even had the nerve to call it! That's rich. I think you *had* a pretty good hand right about then—three-of-a-kind if not better . . . (*Beat.*) How many fathers of how many under-grads were you working on when I met you? All this time, I've had the . . . I dunno what . . . dignity I guess, some last shred of my *self-esteem* to never ever ask you that but I'm asking it now. So. How many guys got a note that year? Hmm?

VELVET You don't wanna know that. Not really.

FRED I do. Now I do.

VELVET No, you don't.

FRED Actually you'd be surprised. Right here at the end, there's like a moment of . . . not quite *clarity*, I wouldn't call it that exactly, but it's something close. Like the sun coming outta the clouds for just a second and reminding us how things used to be. Clear and crisp. And yeah, at this moment . . . as I pick up my bags and I limp off to some Holiday Inn to weep my eyes out like some . . . fucking *first grader* . . . yes. I wanna know. (*Beat.*) How many? Hmm? Round it off if you need to.

VELVET . . . maybe six. Five or six, I guess.

FRED Huh.

VELVET About that many. Not that they all took the offer, but yeah. Probably six.

FRED Wow. Like you kids are prone to saying—wow.

VELVET It didn't seem like that many at the time to me. But it's—yes. I guess it's a lot.

FRED And how many takers? Just for the record.

VELVET Four. More or less. Not full-time, but . . .

FRED Huh. And the other two?

VELVET They never said a word. I got a couple of hang-up calls but nothing else. I mean, what're they gonna say, right?

FRED True.

A moment of détente—still tense but they let the quiet stand for a moment. Silence.

VELVET Come to think of it those boys did start to see me less, fade out a bit so maybe their dads did say something. I dunno and you know what? That's ancient history to me. It's like reading about the Greeks . . .

FRED Not quite. The Greeks liked little boys.

VELVET Ha! Good one, Fred. Nice.

FRED Yeah, I still got it . . . my charm and my small cock.

VELVET I never said *small*. I just didn't build you up with stories about how huge you were . . . believe it or not, I'm not a pro at this—I was always making shit up as I went along.

FRED Yeah, well, you might toss a compliment in there ever so often for a fellow—it does wonders!

VELVET I'll remember that.

FRED I bet you will.

VELVET Anyway . . .

FRED Yeah, anyway, go on, please. So a few of these daddies—old deluded assholes a lot like me—fell for the cute little "GIRL FOR SALE" notice you tucked in each of our pockets and that was it? That's how you paid for tuition and books and shit?

VELVET Pretty much. That and other stuff. Saw Europe one summer, too. And *Morocco*.

FRED "*And* Morocco" she says! Nice! Good! Bully for you.

VELVET It is what it is. I'm not beaming with pride over here.

FRED No, but you're not down on your knees and asking for God's forgiveness now, either, are ya?

VELVET No, guess not.

FRED Nope. You're just somewhere comfortably in-between.

VELVET I s'pose so.

FRED Uh-huh. Like most everybody. We do shit, make an absolute mess of the things going on around us and then we find some way to still get by, to live with ourselves. That's us in a fucking nutshell. People.

She accepts this without letting it be a victory for him.

VELVET Listen, I don't feel like a *murderer*, if that's what you're implying. We were all adults and it was . . . just this . . .

FRED It was obviously a game, that's what it was! More than I ever even realized. So fuck, there's a lesson to be learned . . . I really should've asked about others in the beginning. Probably would've helped me from falling so hard for you . . .

VELVET I hope not. Honestly.

FRED Yeah?

VELVET I feel like—whatever you say now—it was something special that we had, I think. A very unique and—I know it pissed you off that I wouldn't call it . . . what you wanted it to be, a "relationship," which it was, obviously, yes . . . anything can be that, but we never named it in that way that people do. "We're dating" or "he's my boyfriend" or what-not because it just wasn't that . . . not really—it was amazing and sorta changed my life for a while but it wasn't a regular thing. With a name.

FRED No, I get it. You're right. It really did make me mad back then, and I got all . . . (*Beat.*) It was probably the start of the end of things. That whole deal . . . me not knowing what we had, or what to call it. Me wanting to talk about the *future* . . .

VELVET Everybody does that, wants to push and . . . you know. Label shit. That's what we do! I'm not saying it was wrong of you asking for it, but I did try to be clear about why I couldn't do it. At least right then why I couldn't . . . but . . .

FRED Yeah, and now I get it! Because you had a few other proud poppas falling over each other to get into your very tight jeans. It was a pretty good *racket*, I gotta hand it to ya . . .

VELVET It wasn't a racket, Fred. It was a job. It was my after-school job.

FRED Really? That's what I was? Huh. Well, you give great *customer service*, honey . . . and it was worth it to cum in your mouth. It was expensive and humiliating in the end but that part—my shit dripping off your chin each time?—that was totally worth the price of admission. (*Beat.*) Just so we're clear about our "relationship."

VELVET Stop it! You know what I mean.

FRED No, I really don't. It was your "job" but you just sorta *accidentally* fell for me?

VELVET Kinda. Yeah.

FRED That's shit! That's romance novel shit I don't even believe in . . . I mean . . .

VELVET Doesn't matter. It's true.

FRED And the other guys? Not that I care much about second place, but what happened to them? Huh?

VELVET One or two ended up feeling the same way you did— whether I felt that way or not—and we made a mess of things, that's how shit like this can go, it's a risk, but a few of them were great. We'd meet in some hotel or at a spot upstate, once a week, I'd take the train up or wherever and we would, you know . . . we'd do that and I'd be back in class by nightfall. 500 dollars richer than I was that morning. (*Beat.*) It doesn't suck to only work two or . . . three hours a week when you're going to school.

FRED Probably shouldn't use the word "suck" to describe the quality of the experience . . . might get confusing.

VELVET Uh-huh. Make fun if you want to, but it's all just been work and that's the way I look at it. Ok? "Work."

FRED Yeah, well . . . I think maybe you should *look* a little bit harder next time . . .

VELVET So I can see what? That I should've been working in an

Applebee's? Or stripping? Would that've been better, or maybe just strutting my shit at *Hooter's*? Which do you think? (*Beat.*) You use what you have and that's what I did. Still do. Chris gets paid to do computers because he's great with them. You're an attorney and that's your gift. I have tits and all the other stuff that guys want and I'm not sorry that I let men use me once in a while. My mom got *used* all her life . . . every day she was an adult and you know how much she got paid for it? Not even one fucking *dime*, ok? That's how much. (*Beat.*) You can guilt me into saying what I did was wrong but it wasn't . . . not for me. Not then or now. You don't have to like it or . . . understand me but I'm not gonna let you tell me that I've done a bad thing here. I did what I needed to, what suited me at the time and still does . . . from time to time. (*Beat.*) I used to get called a *whore* in school when I was just sitting at my desk or at home if I got there late for dinner—you think it stings more if you say it? "Slut," or "cunt" or any of that shit?! Not now. I got numb to all that years and years ago. Sorry to burst your bubble, Fred.

FRED   Baby . . . my bubble's been burst for so long that it looks like I'm dragging a fucking *tail* behind me.

VELVET   I gotta go, Fred. I do.

FRED   . . . hold up . . .

VELVET   No, I really have to.

FRED   Chris can fucking wait! If he doesn't have to get back to his wife then he's got all the time in the world. He-can-wait.

VELVET   Fine. (*Stands there.*) What else? Ya made me stop so what else do you want?

FRED What else is "what do I do now?" And I'm being completely serious here . . .

VELVET I've already said . . .

FRED I'm *not* going back home! Fuck, I've told you that!

VELVET Alright, fine, stop getting so . . .

FRED Well, then listen! OK? Just listen to me. (*Beat.*) I need some help here. I can't go back to Miriam, whether you and I—that doesn't even play into this. I can't go back to all that! Impossible. So . . .

VELVET Ok, then you . . . something. Do something else with your life. For now. Do like I said; go get some temporary place so you can drop your shit off and just slow it down for a minute. You're practically on some—you're jumping outta your skin and it's driving both of us up the wall here! Just try to *relax* for a minute and . . . this weekend we'll . . . we can get together or . . .

FRED Oh, that's right! You already pencilled me in for "Sunday!" *How* could I forget?

VELVET Hey, we don't have to. I just thought . . .

FRED No, it's great. Something to look forward to, like one of my favorite TV shows. I'm gonna stick it in my *iPhone* just so that I'll be here bright and early. Promise!

VELVET You're being an ass about it now, right? Making fun of me . . .

FRED Sorta.

VELVET Well then fuck it, let's forget it!

FRED Fine! You can ask Chris for some extra cash this week . . .

VELVET Stop bringing him up! Just stop it!!

FRED He's my kid, so I can do any . . .

VELVET . . . and he's my friend! We're *friends* and he likes me a helluva lot more than you!

FRED Ohhh, ouch. That hurt.

VELVET Fuck you.

FRED I wish. But now I'm not so sure—I think I still want to but you're getting less and less attractive by the minute.

VELVET Fred, please, God! Just go now.

FRED Really? And I thought it was all going so well . . .

VELVET *Please.*

FRED Ok. I'm exhausted so why not? We're just going in circles so yeah, maybe I oughta take a break. You do your shit and then call me later. Will ya? Please?

VELVET I will.

FRED Ok. I'll get going, then . . . (*Beat.*) If you gimme a kiss first.

VELVET What?

FRED You heard me.

VELVET Fred.

FRED Oh come on . . . it's just a kiss.

VELVET   No, that's not true.

FRED   'Course it is. A little peck.

VELVET   Not to me. No kiss is just that. Only a kiss. They're always a special thing . . .

FRED   Ok, fine, they're *magic*, I agree! And I want one. Just one more . . . from you.

VELVET   I don't think that's such a good—look, maybe just on the cheek. Ok?

FRED   Fuck the cheek. Sorry, but that's gay. Why don't ya just say "next time I see you I'm gonna give you a massive *hug*" to make me really feel like shit. I want a *kiss*. (*Beat.*) Pro-rate it for me— outta 500 dollars, a kiss should be about what? Maybe 75 bucks, all in? Right?

VELVET   Don't say things like that.

FRED   No, I'm serious. I'm actually asking here, so . . . come on.

VELVET   Stop.

FRED   What? (*Beat.*) *Please*?

VELVET   I'll give you one for free if you'll get the fuck outta here when we finish . . .

FRED   Now there's a deal! Yes, I'll take it . . . (*Beat.*) Whenever you're ready, baby. I'm here for you.

VELVET   Fine. Let's do it. Come over here and kiss me, then . . .

(*They kiss. It falters, then it keeps growing. Finally stops.*) Shit. You always could kiss . . .

FRED You too. My God, I've forgotten just how much.

VELVET Listen . . . (*But he doesn't listen—kissing her again—she responds and it deepens.*) Fred, please . . . I can't do this . . .

FRED No, don't. Don't ruin it. Just give it a second. (*They wait for a moment.*) Not yet. Lemme just . . . soak that in for a . . .

VELVET Ok. (*Waits.*) And now I need to take off . . . honestly. I'm so late!

FRED Right. You almost let me forget. "Wonder boy."

VELVET I asked you about that . . .

FRED Yeah, you know what? I'm gonna let him bring it up before I cease and desist, ok? He hates it so much, let *him* tell me.

VELVET You're really awful sometimes.

FRED Only when I'm awake.

VELVET No, not just then . . .

FRED Ha! Good one. Right at the heart.

VELVET You've earned it.

FRED So go then, if you need to so badly. I'll be right behind you. Scout's honor.

VELVET Fine. Lemme just— (*Starts to gather her things.*) Do lock it, though. Promise?

FRED I do. I promise.

VELVET Cool. I'll see you soon. Maybe Sunday.

FRED Hope so. I'd like that.

VELVET Me, too.

FRED Would you really?

VELVET I think. If it happens naturally, then yes. I would.

FRED What's "naturally" mean? Just so I know. With or without a *condom*? (*Beat.*) Kidding! Seriously. You tell me.

VELVET Start again as whatever, friends or . . .

FRED Us? "Friends?"

VELVET Yeah, why not?

FRED A million reasons. I can even write 'em down for you if ya want me to . . .

VELVET That's not—we used to be good around each other, just being near the other person was enough. Don't you remember? I would light up in a second, right as you came into a room? *Remember?*

FRED That's true.

VELVET So, then, that's what I'd like. To be a bit more like that to start, and then . . .

FRED What? (*Beat.*) *What?*

VELVET We'll see! God, you keep nudging me even when we're just talking about it. Don't you feel that? (Beat.) We talk for two seconds about it, take a baby step forward . . . and immediately we're at *Tiffany's* picking a ring out! Just stop! Cool it . . . please. I really can't *deal* with the . . . whole . . .

FRED I can't help it! Sorry! It's how you make me feel—I've *never* felt that with other women. So full of . . . everything. Love and pain and jealousy. You make me feel that shit again. Like I was seventeen . . .

VELVET I guess that's . . . nice or something.

FRED It was meant to be, yeah.

VELVET Then thank you. Thanks.

FRED My first girlfriend, I mean, first big one—not just some kid from class—she made me so jealous one summer; she and her family went off to the *Bahamas* or somewhere and they had this older guy with 'em, a family friend who was . . . anyway. Some fucker. This thirty-year-old fucker got after her and she let him . . . so I start calling their condo every day for a month, over and over until her dad finally got on the phone and was yelling at me, had to call my mom to stop me . . . and in the end I had rung up a thousand dollar phone bill. Seriously, one *thousand* dollars . . . which back then was, like . . . well, huge. I had to work a solid year at a local store to pay that off. But what I'm saying is, she was the last person who made me feel like that. In fact . . . I wouldn't even let myself be that way with another person. Ever. Until we met. You stirred all that shit up in me again. *(Beat.)* So.

VELVET Well, that's . . . but that's not what I can do right now. Anything like that, I mean, of that *magnitude*. You understand?

FRED Yes. I do. (*Beat.*) But we can try? Can't we? I mean, just see how it goes? (*Beat.*) Isn't that even . . . remotely . . . ?

VELVET Maybe.

FRED Between us. That's possible, isn't it? It can be like you say, short steps ahead if you want but yeah, forward. Not just in, like, circles, 'cause that'll kill me . . .

VELVET Maybe. If you don't push things. Push *me*.

FRED Ok.

VELVET If you take it easy.

FRED I can do that . . .

VELVET And at regular hours. Daytime hours at first.

FRED You mean "lunch?"

VELVET Yes. I do. And not in code—just food.

FRED Ok.

VELVET Maybe then.

FRED Alright. (*Beat.*) Anything else?

VELVET No, just . . . things like that.

FRED Really? No other rules for me? Any other guidelines I need to follow so I can be allowed into your *presence*?

VELVET . . . Fred . . .

FRED Just wanna be clear! I mean, God! You're so fucking *cold* to me now . . . it's just . . .

VELVET Forget it. I'm going.

FRED No, come on, I'm kidding! When did you stop being able to take a fucking joke? Seriously, when?

VELVET Right around the time they stopped being funny . . .

FRED Nice one! Yes! BAM!! You're a lot faster than you used to be.

VELVET Hey, I learned from the best.

FRED I hope that means "me."

VELVET I was referring to Chris, actually.

FRED Another one! Right to the chest. POW! (*Beat.*) Luckily it's a lie. That kid's many things—funny is not one of 'em. (*Phone rings, he checks it.*) Fuck.

VELVET The wife?

FRED Indeed. That won't be the last time.

VELVET Maybe you should answer it. Just as a surprise . . .

FRED Maybe it's none of your business.

VELVET Go on.

FRED *Maybe* I will . . .

VELVET I doubt that. Not with me here. (*Beat.*) You like to keep your little worlds all nice and separate. Always have.

FRED Don't worry about it! Stop now.

VELVET No, go ahead. I dare you. You made me do it in front of you, so your turn now . . .

FRED Just— (*Snaps phone shut.*) I said you can leave, so go.

VELVET Oh, thanks very much! Yeah? I can leave?

FRED I wouldn't push it so much. Just go.

VELVET No, you know what? I don't feel so good about leaving you here, with all my . . .

FRED Don't worry, I'm not gonna steal any of your shit. IKEA's not really my bag . . . I tend to spend more than ten bucks a piece on my dining room chairs.

VELVET And what's to steal? Right? Half the shit in this place you bought for me . . .

FRED I *didn't* buy those chairs! No way.

VELVET You know what I'm saying . . .

FRED Yes. Are you saying I spoiled you?

VELVET A little.

FRED Or are you implying that I *bought* your love? Which?

VELVET Both, probably.

FRED Well, well, that's ugly and sordid.

VELVET It is what it is.

FRED Yeah, you said that before and it bugged me then so try another phrase, ok? You're not Mark Twain so you don't need to be so fucking *folksy* about everything . . . plain ol' English is fine by me.

VELVET You've got a *retort* for everything, now, don't ya, Fred?

FRED Just about. Except for maybe you using the word "retort." That sort of speaks for itself . . .

VELVET God! Once a prick . . .

FRED . . . always a prick. Luckily it works that way with both genders but I will refrain from name-calling. For the moment.

She springs up and moves over to the front door. Points.

VELVET You need to leave. *Now.* (*Beat.*) I've been nice—tried to be, anyhow—and now I have to get on the road. So come on.

FRED Again with the threats.

VELVET It's not a fucking . . . it's a fact! Okay?! Simple goddamn fact that I need to leave now!!

FRED Fine. Let's go. You just gotta ask *nice.* (*Goes to his bags and begins collecting them.*) Help me out?

VELVET Sure.

FRED Maybe throw that one up here and then I can get those . . . (*He reaches for her.*) I just want one more kiss.

VELVET No, stop it!

FRED You stop . . . it's just a kiss . . .

VELVET Stop! Don't!

FRED Oh, fuck, don't be so . . . !

VELVET Fred! No!! Let go of me!!

FRED Come here, just . . . quit fighting me!!

VELVET STOP IT!!

They grapple for a moment—she bites down on his hand.

FRED Goddamnit, you bit me! Oww, you fucking little—kiss me!
You *owe* me that much!!

VELVET I don't *owe* you anything! Get off! STOP!!

FRED YOU STOP!! I'M JUST TRYING TO . . . !!

VELVET Help! Someone help me!! Stop!!! STOP!!!

FRED Shut up! Shut up!! You shut your goddamn mouth!!! SHUT
UP!!!!

*This next part should be long and ugly and brutal—it's a rape,
there's no way around that fact—so it needs to be as real and
drawn-out as possible.*

*Furniture should get overturned, some things broken, etc. In the
end* FRED *is on top—literally—and he fucks* VELVET *from behind.*

*It's a Pyrrhic victory at best. She gives as good as she gets. This
should be pushed as far as possible, with all the noise and words
that help them reach that difficult place.*

*As the smoke clears, he gets to his feet, pulls up his slacks, then
gathers himself. A long silence drops in.* VELVET *is left sobbing on
the floor.*

FRED Say "hi" to Chris for me.

He goes to pick up his belongings but leaves a lot of the bags on the ground. Picks up his two suitcases.

And with that he goes out the door. Silence. Only sound is her slowly ebbing tears.

After a long moment, he walks back into the room, with his suitcases in tow. What the fuck?

Surprise.

The following exchange is very business-like. They are almost like two different people now. They are, in fact.

> . . . hey there. (*Beat.*) You ok?

VELVET Hey. (*Stops crying.*) Fuck. Geez.

FRED I know.

VELVET I mean, seriously. Shit! (*Beat.*) Glad it's Sunday and a lot of my neighbors go out for the . . . 'cause we were pretty . . . Jesus!

FRED I know! I hear ya.

VELVET That was . . . you know? *Intense.*

FRED Yeah! God, sorry, if I . . . was . . .

VELVET No, it's fine. It was amazing.

FRED Thanks. You, too.

VELVET Of course.

FRED No, seriously! Thanks. I'm still . . .

VELVET Sure. Did I catch you with an elbow?

FRED Ummm, I'm not sure—whole thing was sort of a blur, at the end there. It's . . .

VELVET No shit! And I was really struggling, not faking it. I was. Fighting you.

FRED I could feel that. Thanks. Felt good.

VELVET 'Course.

FRED . . . a couple times, I really did think you got, I dunno, not pissed at me but, like, caught up in the . . . whole . . .

VELVET I did! I totally did! Yes!

FRED Yeah? Me, too!

VELVET Completely! (*Beat.*) And by the way, not a word to anybody about the "no condom" thing, okay? Seriously. That's just between you and me.

FRED Of course! I mean . . . God. Yes. *Sure.*

VELVET Good. (*Smiles.*) Ha! Some of the shit you said, to me . . . Jesus Christ, *where'd* you come up with that?! Ya know?

FRED I dunno! Just a very . . . *vivid* imagination, I guess. (*Beat.*) Try sitting at a desk all day! You'll dream up some . . . crazy . . .

VELVET No thanks! (*Smiles.*) The "desk job," I'm saying. No thank you.

FRED Of course. I just meant—nothing. (*Pulls a bank envelope out of his pocket.*) Anyway, here. Go ahead and check . . . is this enough? For all the . . . ?

VELVET It's what we agreed to. Right?

FRED Yes, with a little bit of a tip there. Oh wait— (*Gives her some extra bills.*) For the *candlestick* thingies. Sorry, not planned!

VELVET Thank you. And no worries—they're just some shit from, you know, Crate & Barrel. The agency will replace them . . .

FRED Good! (*Beat.*) Can I use your . . . ummmm, you know what? Nothing. (*Checking watch.*) It's kinda late, we even went over a bit, so I'll go. Are you sure you're . . . ?

VELVET I'm cool. Really. I would've stopped you if I'd wanted to.

FRED Ok, great. Good! That's . . .

VELVET Anyway.

FRED Yeah, anyway. I'll . . . (*Beat.*) I still need to drop all this crap off at the *Goodwill* on my way back!

VELVET Ha!

FRED I know, pathetic, right? (Laughs.) If only our loved ones could see us for what we really are—nobody'd ever sleep again!

VELVET I *know*, right?

FRED It's true.

VELVET I'm not arguing with ya. (*Goes to him.*) You want me to help you load up?

FRED That'd be great . . .

VELVET Here— (*Puts a bag or two over his arm.*) I can't believe you dragged all this up to my place!

FRED   Well, I've got the car, so it's just . . . hey, it's exercise! That's how I looked at it.

VELVET   Right.

FRED   Not so bad. And now it's all downstairs, so I'm fine.
No worries.

VELVET   'Kay. Sure? I can . . .

FRED   No, please! You should just—I'll be ok and I really do have to run. (*Beat.*) I've got the twins this weekend so I need to get back for the neighbor girl who's . . .

VELVET   Fine, then. Go for it.

FRED   Thanks. (*Phone rings.*) Damn! Hold on.

VELVET   *Miriam*?

FRED   Ha! No, the sitter again—I'll call back.

VELVET   Okay. And . . . are you good for . . . what about next time?
On the phone you said . . .

FRED   Oh, yeah, I just needed to—don't laugh at me, but I think I'm on vacation during the date we set. Sorry!

VELVET   Really? Just you or . . . ?

FRED   Yeah. Well, kids and me. Their mom's off on some other deal, I can't keep up with her schedule. I can *pay* for it, of course, but I can't keep up with it!

VELVET   Ha! I've heard that one before.

FRED I bet! (*Beat.*) I just mean . . . shit. Sorry. I didn't mean to . . . anyway, yeah, we're off to the, ummmm . . . for a week or so.

VELVET Where? The *Bahamas*?

FRED Ahhh . . . (*Grins.*) Yes, you got me. Yes. And I didn't mean to use it during the—that was a mistake, I'm very very sorry.

VELVET Ha! Well, at least now I know where some of it comes from . . . God . . .

FRED Sorry! That was—I shouldn't've used that today, it's a little bit creepy.

VELVET Don't worry about it . . . (*Beat.*) And I like how I get the same profession all the time but you end up a *lawyer*! Nice one!

FRED No, stop! That just slipped out and, so, so, yeah, I just went with it. But . . .

VELVET . . . sure . . .

FRED Honestly! (*Beat.*) Now I feel bad. This is all meant to be an escape, not some—and you're also an *actress*, right? You said that before . . . but you just haven't . . . you know what I'm trying to say!

VELVET I'm kidding! It's alright. It is. (*Checks watch.*) 'S getting late.

FRED Right!

VELVET So take care. And we'll figure out next time . . .

FRED Next time. (*Beat.*) "Worry about now right now." Isn't that what you said before? You taught me that.

VELVET I did. And it's true.

FRED Then I will. Anyhow . . . thanks, again. It was really . . . something else! So amazing and . . . just . . . yes. That. *Amazing.*

VELVET I agree. Thank *you.* (Beat.) You'll call?

FRED I will.

VELVET Promise?

FRED I do. Soon.

VELVET Good. I'll be here.

FRED Ok, then . . . so have a great . . . so long.

VELVET Take it easy. "Fred."

FRED Sorry! What a lame name, right?

VELVET No, I thought it was cute.

FRED Really?

VELVET I did. Yes. (*Smiles.*) And mine, too . . . "Velvet." Ha! That was classic.

FRED Oh, good! I'm glad. It was my great-grandmother's nickname. I'd rather not discuss it . . . (*Smiles.*) Yeah. Ok, then.

VELVET Weird, but, hey. (*Smiles.*) Ok. So . . .

FRED Yes. Thanks, and . . . yeah. 'Bye.

VELVET G'bye. "Fred."

FRED Ha! G'bye. "Velvet."

An actual kiss this time but only on the cheek. A smile between them and a long hug and then he goes out again, weighted down with his many bags. He is gone.

She stands staring at the door for a long time in silence. A strange look on her face.

Finally, she goes back to the couch. Puts on an oversized set of headphones. Closes her eyes and lets the music overtake her as the world melts slowly away.

Silence. Darkness.

In the companion piece to Neil LaBute's 2009 Tony-nominated *Reasons to be Pretty*, Greg, Steph, Carly, and Kent pick up their lives three years later, but in different romantic pairings, as they each search desperately for that elusive object of desire: happiness.

"Mr. LaBute is more relaxed as a playwright than he's ever been. He is clearly having a good time revisiting old friends . . . you're likely to feel the same way . . . the most winning romantic comedy of the summer, replete with love talk, LaBute-style, which isn't so far from hate talk . . . " —**Ben Brantley**, *The New York Times*

$14.95 978-1-4683-0721-4

THE OVERLOOK PRESS • NEW YORK • WWW.OVERLOOKPRESS.COM

Betty and Bobby are sister and brother, but they have little in common. She's a college professor with a prim demeanor, and he's a carpenter with a foul mouth and violent streak. Yet on the night when Betty urgently needs help to empty her cabin in the woods—the cabin she's been renting to a male student—she calls on Bobby. In this exhilarating play of secrets and sibling rivalry, Neil LaBute unflinchingly explores the dark territory beyond, as Bobby sneeringly says, "the lies you tell yourself to get by."

"Very much a meditation on what is and is not true . . . and also a further manifestation of the longstanding authorial fascination with the close link between deep intimacy and dark violence."
                                                                        —*Chicago Tribune*

$14.95 978-1-4683-0704-7

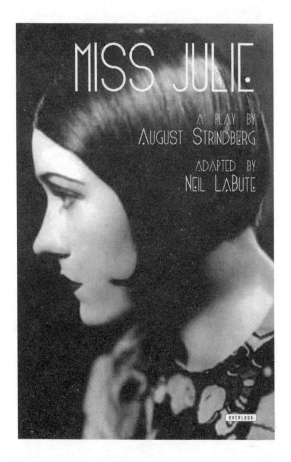

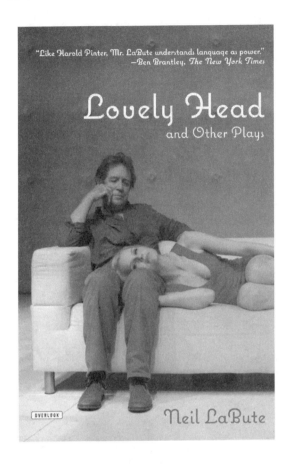

"Like Harold Pinter, Mr. LaBute understands language as power."
—Ben Brantley, The New York Times

Lovely Head
and Other Plays

Neil LaBute

The title play, which had its American premiere at La MaMa in 2012, rivetingly explores the relationship between a nervous older man and a glib young prostitute, as their evening together drives toward a startling conclusion.

Also included is the one-act play *The Great War*, which looks at a divorcing couple and the ground they need to cross to reach their own end of hostilities; *In the Beginning*, which was written as a response to the Occupy movement and produced around the world in 2012-13 as part of *Theatre Uncut*; *The Wager*, the stage version of the film *Double or Nothing* starring Adam Brody; the two-handers *A Guy Walks Into a Bar, Over the River and Through the Woods,* and *Strange Fruit;* and two powerful new monologues, *Bad Girl* and *The Pony of Love.*

€16.95 978-1-4683-0705-4

Neil LaBute burst onto the American theater scene in 1999 with the premiere of *bash* at NYC's Douglas Fairbanks Theater. These three provocative one-act plays, which examine the complexities of evil in everyday life, thrillingly exhibit LaBute's signature raw lyrical intensity. In *Medea Redux*, a woman tells of her complex and ultimately tragic relationship with her grade school English teacher; in *Iphigenia in Orem,* a Utah businessman confides in a stranger in a Las Vegas hotel room, confessing a most chilling crime; and in *A Gaggle of Saints*, a young Mormon couple separately recounts the violent events of an anniversary weekend in New York City.

"Mr. LaBute shows not only a merciless ear for contemporary speech but also a poet's sense of recurring, slyly graduated imagery . . . darkly engrossing."

—Ben Brantley, ***The New York Times***

$14.95 978-1-58567-024-6